AIMEE'S GIFT

Kathleen Sprout

Proverb Press

ISBN-13 978-0615454238
ISBN-10 0615454232

Cover design
Copyright © robmckay/dreamstime.com

Other books by Kathleen Sprout

Shopping for a Groom - print version   ISBN-13 978-0615454238

CHAPTER ONE

The telephone rang shrilly, jarring Luke from a deep sleep. He opened one eye and fumbled for the receiver, knocking a book off the nightstand. "Uh, hello." Apprehension coursed through him as he glanced at his digital alarm clock and realized it was well after midnight.

"Hello?" Luke couldn't think of any reason for a middle of the night call. Unless . . . *Lord, please don't let Dad take a turn for the worse.*

"Mr. Forsythe?" A soft voice on the other end of the line asked.

"This is Luke Forsythe. Who is this?"

"Mr. Forsythe, I'm calling because I don't have anyone else to call. You've got to help!"

"What is it you want, miss?" Luke was nearly awake. His brain was already scrolling through its memory bank, trying to detect if the low husky feminine voice could be connected to a name or a face he knew.

"There's a man being beaten. He's at the end of Cherry Orchard Road. You have to go there and stop it!"

Luke sighed. She'd dialed the wrong number. "Lady, I don't know who you are or why you think I can help. If this is an emergency, Call 911. The police handle things like that."

"No! You've got to do it! Please, I'm afraid he's going to be killed!"

Luke heard the woman's voice crack. He felt guilty for snapping at her and almost wished he could reach out his hand to give some comfort. But why had she called *him* for help. He was a newspaper columnist, not a cop. And who was she anyway? Did he know her?

"Please! You have to help him yourself!" Even though her words were spoken barely above a whisper, there was no mistaking the urgency.

"Okay, okay, lady. I'll do what I can. What was your name again?" Luke heard a click, followed by a dial tone. Luke groaned, "Why did I ever agree to help?" Had he fallen for some kind of scam and was about to be mugged or burglarized if he left the apartment? Besides, if someone really were in danger, why would he want to jump into the middle of it? Yet, she seemed desperate.

He quickly pulled on his sweats and shoved his bare feet inside a pair of running shoes. Outside his apartment he sent up a quick prayer of thanks that the phone call had not delivered bad news about his father.

Pulling away from his apartment complex in his all-wheel-drive mini-van, he focused his attention on trying to remember the location of Cherry Orchard Road.

He drove north from Wenatchee, along the Columbia River. Finally he spotted the road and turned left and headed uphill, away from the river.

Luke squinted his eyes as his headlights punched two holes through the October fog. He hoped if anyone really was in trouble, the man, whoever he was, could wait for him to slowly wind his way up the narrow road. He had the eerie sensation he was getting into something way over his head, and wished he had remembered to grab his cell phone. Doubt flooded over him, making him want to return to the warm comfort of his bed.

He sighed in relief to see a deputy sheriff's vehicle parked at the end of the road. Luke stopped nearby, leaving his engine idling. A young Hispanic man sat cross-legged in the road. The headlights of Luke's vehicle illuminated his face, revealing a trickle of blood leaking from above his right eye and dripping down over a sullen expression to fall on the collar of a faded and torn cotton shirt. Luke felt immediate pity for the young man and surmised that this was probably the one that his mysterious caller had told him about. He pushed the button to lower the window on his door.

"Hey You!" A brash voice called out of the darkness. "If you don't have any business here, I'd advise you to move along!"

"I just came to see if I could help." Luke peered through the darkness, trying to see who he was talking to. The sound of footsteps crunching on the gravel road told him the man who had called out and who he assumed was the officer, was quickly approaching.

"Everything is under control here. These folks get in squabbles all the time." The deputy approached Luke's door and shined his flashlight into the mini-van, arcing the light from Luke's face, to the passenger seat, the rear compartment and back again. "What are you doing up here at this time of night?"

"I got a phone call. Someone said that there was a man in trouble up here."

"There're no phones around here. You'd better let us handle our job. We don't need people getting in the way. Who did you say called you?" The deputy still held the beam of his Maglite on Luke's face, making it nearly impossible to see.

'I don't know who it was. The person hung up." How much information was he required to give to the deputy? After all, he couldn't exactly claim he was a reporter protecting his news sources. "Is that fellow going to be all right? Does he need medical attention?"

"He's fine. Like I said, this happens all the time up here. Not worth your worrying about. Now I suggest you get on your way. There's nothing for you to do here." The deputy abruptly turned and walked over to the man who had not moved from his sitting position on the gravel road. He reached down, taking the man by the elbow and helped him to his feet.

Luke knew when he wasn't wanted, so discreetly backed his van around and left.

At the bottom of the hill he pulled up to the stop sign, putting his right-turn signal on before turning onto the paved road. A movement in the adjacent orchard caught his eye. The fog was thicker now. It distorted even the outline of the fence. He could have sworn he saw the dark figure of a woman floating among the cherry trees. Luke rubbed his left eye and yawned. Chalking the evening up to a waste of time, he turned his attention to staying out of the ditch and getting home in one piece.

***

Quinton Partlow, editor of the Wenatchee Morning Word, leaned back in his leather chair, eyes half closed. His hands and fingers formed a steeple over his portly stomach. Luke watched his boss gaze benevolently at the group seated around the walnut conference table. Partlow did this at the conclusion of each staff meeting, giving the impression that he was contemplating great things and about to give a word of wisdom to his less enlightened employees. He never did, though. In fact, nothing he ever said surprised anyone who had worked for him for any length of time.

For some of Luke's co-workers at the small Eastern Washington newspaper, the editor's lack of forward thinking was a blessing. No stress, no pressure, just everyone plodding along doing their job. Of course, the paper couldn't begin to compete with the larger city newspapers, but still, it maintained a small but loyal readership.

The meeting was over and Luke waited for the others to leave. He was anxious to run an idea past Partlow, the man who had hired him just six months ago.

"Luke." Partlow's mouth barely moved as he spoke to the younger man. "You're doing a fine job writing that column of yours."

"I want to talk to you about that. I've got some ideas I'd like to explore."

4

"I'm willing to listen to any of your ideas, Luke. Just as long as you don't change the flavor of the column. I think you've seen the letters that our readers send in. Your column makes them feel real good."

"Well, I'm wondering if we're doing our readers a favor. Perhaps we should get them thinking more. You know . . . get them to want to *do* good, not merely *feel* good."

Partlow's face remained a mask of impassiveness. "What exactly did you have in mind, Luke?"

"I was up on Cherry Orchard Road last night and saw-"

"Cherry Orchard Road?" Partlow's voice raised a notch. "What on earth would one of my people be doing up there?"

"I was just trying to explain, sir. I got this call in the middle of the night to go there and help someone." Luke wondered if Partlow's proprietary attitude toward his employees extended to their free time as well.

"Who was the call from?"

"A woman . . . a young woman, judging from the sound of her voice. Anyway, I drove up there, just on a whim, and there was a Mexican man who had been in some kind of fight." Luke stopped, realizing he wasn't making sense and shuffled his papers. Judging by Partlow's demeanor, the older man wasn't in the least interested in what Luke had to say.

The editor let out a big sigh. "And what does any of this have to do the Morning Word?"

"Well," Luke slowly said, his mind racing ahead to form the words that would sway his boss, "I'd like to go up there again and interview some of the people who work in the orchards."

"Whatever for?" Partlow sat straight up in his chair. "Our readers don't want to hear about any of those people up there. It would be a waste of your time, and the paper's resources."

"Well, I just thought, sir, that with the holidays coming up, that people would want to know how they could help someone less fortunate than themselves. Maybe organize a food drive or something."

Luke's boss stood and moved around the table. Slapping his hand on Luke's shoulder as he passed, he said, "Nobody cares about that. There are plenty of other charities around people can contribute to. Besides, they take care of their own. Take it from me. They don't want any of us interfering in their business. Just keep on writing the columns like you've done in the past, boy. You'll make us all happy."

Luke wasn't exactly stunned that his boss turned down his idea. The paper was famous for maintaining its status-quo. He just wished he had known the paper's reputation before he took the job.

He gathered up the notes he had taken at the meeting. *He's wrong. Somebody does care. The Lord cares about those people. And that woman cared enough to call a complete stranger last night. Who is she? Wife? Mother? Sister?*

Luke strode down the hall to his little cubicle of an office, and sat to type the next day's "feel-good" piece for the newspaper. He typed out a nonsensical humorous segment about beautifying the city's parks then picked up the phone to check his voice-mail.

"Hi Lukie, it's Mom. Just wanted to let you know that Dad had his checkup this morning and he's holding his own. The doctor thinks this new heart medicine will take away some of the chest pain your Dad's been having. I'll call you later, honey. Bye."

Luke let out a huge sigh. He'd wanted to return to Chicago when his father had first started experiencing health problems, but his parents wouldn't hear of it. They were both in their sixties but had always been in excellent health. Until recently. Luke felt guilty that they were going through this alone. This wasn't the first time he doubted the wisdom of his move out to Washington State. He pressed the button to listen to the next message.

"Luke! Pastor Greg here. I'm calling to see if we're still on for breakfast this Saturday. Call me."

"Beep."

"Mr. Forsythe? I want to thank you for what you did last night. I knew you were a good man and would help even if you don't know me. Anyway . . . thanks. Uh, bye."

"It's her!" Luke punched the key to repeat the message. He listened to the message three times, memorizing each inflection in her voice. *She sounds young. Her voice has a sweet huskiness to it . . . kinda like Debra Winger, the movie star. A very pretty voice today and not fearful sounding like in the first call. No accent that I can detect. I wish she'd call back.*

Luke looked at his Rolex, the same one his parents had given him when he graduated from the University in Illinois. There was still time to drive back to Cherry Orchard Road before it got dark. He grabbed his corduroy sports jacket, a notebook from his desk, and left the building.

***

Aimee McPherson flexed her shoulders, trying to loosen the muscles in her back after the hours she'd spent in front of her computer screen. She waited as the color printer clicked and whirred, letting her know her newest creation neared completion. Her fingers caught the brightly colored papers from the printer and she knew as she looked at each piece that this was one of her best efforts yet.

Who would have thought that anyone could actually make a living creating greeting cards? Well, not a fantastic income, but enough to pay the rent, buy food, and stash the rest in a growing savings account. *And* it provided her the seclusion she required as well. She felt satisfied. Working toward her goal with the end in sight did that to a person.

She carefully placed her newest verse and graphic designs in a manila envelope after addressing it to her faceless publisher of four years. It never ceased to amaze her that she had developed a friendship with Mrs. Crow, a woman she'd never met. But then, they each had something the other wanted. Wasn't that what most relationships were made of? She wondered how many friends Mrs. Crow had and if she knew that she was Aimee's only friend.

Someday that all would change. Someday, she would have lots of friends. Maybe even a boyfriend and eventually a husband and family. But not now. It was out of the question to wish for it or even think about it now.

A buzzing from the small kitchenette let Aimee know her food was done. She'd treated herself to a frozen gourmet dinner as a reward for completing her project on time. The fragrance of shrimp fettuccini rose in a cloud of steam as she pulled the aluminum plate out of the oven and carried it to the small table.

Aimee sat down, opened the latest issue of the Wenatchee Morning Word and studied the photo of the new humor journalist. Her gaze absorbed the fuzzy details of the black and white picture of Luke Forsythe.

Now that's what I'd like my future husband to look like. Short crisp blond hair, a nice smile, clean shaven . . . and he's just as nice as he looks, too. I can tell by the way he writes. He has a good soul. I knew he would help last night. I should think of a way to thank him. On the other hand, it's probably best if I just dropped it.

Aimee savored the last bites of her lonely supper

***

Luke drove back to the spot he'd been directed to the night before. It looked different in the daylight. Not better . . . different. The road ended just beyond the place he had stopped and talked to the deputy. Just past that, were several rows of unpainted wooden shacks. A few olive skinned toddlers were playing with a mangy dog in a yard littered with refuse and car parts. Not a blade of grass in sight. Not anything like the places that he'd played as a child.

An old woman came to the door of one of the houses and stared at Luke's vehicle. She had a baby on one hip and called out something in Spanish to the children he'd noticed earlier. The children reluctantly left their games and entered the house. The woman shut the door behind them without another glance toward Luke.

The sight of the children touched him . . . made him sad. He had never seen, firsthand anyway, a collection of poorer dressed kids in his life. Some of these kids weren't even wearing shoes. He'd heard, of course, about the migrant farm workers that came this far north each year to help with the fruit harvest. He hadn't realized the families came along, too.

The rumbling noise of a diesel engine reached Luke's ears long before the source came into view. He turned his vehicle around and edged over to the side of the gravel road. A former school bus of undetermined age approached. Crowded with men, women and children as young as eight or ten years old, it stopped in front of the shacks. Luke guessed they were all coming home from their work in the orchards. He smiled and waved at them as they disembarked from the bus. Not one person waved in return. By the time the old bus emptied, most of the people had disappeared into their homes. If you could call these rundown buildings homes.

Luke sat there for awhile in the dwindling light. For several years, he'd been praying and asking God for two things. The first request was that God would direct him to a lay ministry that would be important and give meaning to his life. The second request was that God would provide him with a life's partner before he turned thirty. He would be turning thirty this next Christmas Eve, just a couple of months away. No wife in sight. Not even a steady girlfriend.

9

He knew one thing for sure. His life was not taking the path he had always planned. However, maybe these families at the end of Cherry Orchard Road were the answer to his first prayer.

***

Down at the bottom of the hill, Aimee carefully picked the last tomatoes from her meticulously tended vines. Soon the frost would get them and then the snows would come. By then, all but the winter squash, pumpkins, and the last of the potatoes would be harvested and either given away, or put into jars for the winter. Her vegetable garden was a source of pride. Every time she sank her fingers in the warm soil as she pulled the weeds, her heart swelled with a sense of accomplishment and belonging with the earth. How angry her father would be to hear her bragging over her harvest, even to herself. *Pride goeth before a fall. Well, Daddy, you were right. Just see how far I've fallen. But you're not going to rob me of this simple pleasure.*

Several brown grocery bags, full of the fruits of her labor, surrounded her as she knelt in the hand-tilled garden. Aimee stood and carried them one by one to the enclosed back porch of her tiny rented cottage. She then carefully packed them into her bicycle saddle bags. When the bags were full, she filled a cardboard box that would sit in the cargo basket that hung from the handlebars.

The bicycle usually stood in the garage, next to an older model sedan. She only took the sedan out during her monthly trips to Wenatchee to pick up a few groceries and supplies for her work. She had nowhere else to go.

It was just as well. Driving made her uncomfortable. Driving in inclement weather was pure torture. Besides, she preferred to save her precious earnings rather than spend it foolishly on gasoline. There were very few things she needed that she couldn't get through the mail.

Aimee waited until darkness fell before opening the garage door and taking her bike out. Dressed in dark jeans and a navy pea jacket she'd purchased at a surplus store, she easily blended into the shadows as she pumped her way up the hill with her garden's bounty. A dark colored brimmed wool felt hat and a hand-knit scarf covered her long dark hair and hid her face from view. The icy breeze made her eyes water and she was glad she'd dressed to ward off the chill of the night air.

Smoke from the chimneys greeted her as she approached the small Hispanic community. Many families had already left for the South, but this last handful of families had stayed, hoping for the few jobs available at the end of the season. Aimee paused as she spotted two dogs coming toward her. Relieved that they recognized her and were approaching with their tails wagging, she dismounted from her bike, and placed a bag of tomatoes on the porch of the first house. She didn't knock on the door, but moved from house to house until all the bags had been delivered. After patting the dogs on the head, she quietly left with her bike and rode back the way she had come. *Next time I should bring some bones or a treat for the dogs.*

Back home at her desk, she shook out her long hair, running her fingers through the strands that had been plastered down by the old fedora. Her fingers brushed her cheek as she groomed herself, causing her to pause. Tilting her chin downward, she carefully arranged her locks to hang symmetrically over each shoulder.

Reaching for her colored pens, she began composing a note to Mr. Luke Forsythe. Her hands quickly drew a series of birds and flowers around the edge of the note paper.

"No," she said aloud, "this is much too feminine for a man." She set that sheet aside, planning to use it for a note to Mrs. Crow. It wouldn't do to waste paper just because it didn't suit her current need.

11

What should she say? Should she thank him for joining her in her penance for her sins? Tell him that his acts of kindness will be written on tablets on high to be read on the future day of reckoning? No, surely Mr. Forsythe had nothing to atone for.

She opened her top desk drawer and took out the newspaper photograph she had cut out of that day's Morning Word. She taped it to the wall above her computer monitor and turned her thoughts back to the moment she'd called him. She hadn't wanted to, but she hadn't known what else to do. There was no doubt now. She'd done the right thing. He'd come hadn't he? And he'd saved an innocent man from severe injury, if not worse.

Did he expect some kind of payment? Her mind made up, she penned a short thank-you note and tucked it into a small mailing box along with a jar of apricot preserves.

A person should be rewarded for their good deeds . . . as surely as they are punished for their evilness. Would that bad man be punished? Before he did something else? Maybe he was too powerful. The thought both angered and frightened her.

CHAPTER TWO

Luke sat in the coffee shop with his friend, Greg Morton. They tried to make a habit of meeting for breakfast each Saturday.

Greg was one of five pastors who served at one of the largest churches in Wenatchee and had befriended Luke soon after the younger man moved to the area from out of state and joined the church. He was in charge of discipleship at the church and Luke found him to be an intuitive man, skilled at dealing with all kinds of people. They gave their orders to the waitress and made customary small talk as they always did while sipping their first cups of coffee. More important subjects usually were held till after their plates were clean. Today was an exception.

"Luke, you seem excited about something. Care to talk about it?"

Luke didn't need much encouragement to tell the other man all about the incident of a few nights before on Cherry Orchard Road. "And I'm just sure," he continued, his face and hands becoming more animated as he spoke, "that the Lord is directing me to those people up there. The question is . . . what am I supposed to do? They don't seem very friendly. I don't even know a word of Spanish. Yet . . . I feel pulled toward them. Does this seem like a crazy idea to you?" He looked to his friend for advice, knowing he could trust the words he waited for.

"I believe if you are honestly seeking God's direction, it will be revealed to you, if you are just patient."

"Patient? I think I've been pretty patient up until now but it seems like I'm running low on patience these days. I'm almost thirty years old. My life doesn't seem to have any clear direction. In fact it's not turning out anything like I'd hoped for. I've asked God to bring me a woman for a life's

13

partner. There's still no one in sight and I've dated every eligible woman in the church between the ages of twenty and thirty-five. Not one of them shares the same goals as I do, even though most of them come from similar backgrounds. Even my mom has been dropping hints that she'd like to see me settled down."

"Whoa!" Luke's sounding board chuckled as he interrupted the younger man's tirade. "Is this about finding a woman, helping the poor, or discovering God's will?"

Abashed, Luke took a breath and answered, "I guess you hit a hot button when you suggested I need to be patient. It's just . . . my Dad is having heart problems. I'm their only child, and as I watch both my parents get older, I realize that I won't have them around forever. They naturally want to see me settled. Their whole lives have revolved around trying to do their best for me. But . . . I feel like my life is going nowhere."

"That seems like a reasonable thing for parents to want." The gray-haired man across from him reached for a piece of toast and liberally spread it with jelly.

"It's what I want, too, Greg. I just thought it would have happened long before now." Luke turned his head and looked out the window. The coffee shop was filled with the sounds of patrons' voices and clinking dishes as the waitresses bustled from table to table. He suddenly felt homesick. Other than these breakfasts with Greg, and an occasional potluck at church, most of his meals had become a solitary event, meant more for sustenance rather than pleasure. Definitely not times for family sharing. He missed that. He turned back to his plate and moved his hash browns around with his fork. "I've been thinking of moving back to Illinois."

The pastor swallowed and looked directly into his face. "I guess I'm surprised to hear you say that, Luke. Have you forgotten why you moved this far away from your childhood home?"

"No, I haven't forgotten. I really needed to feel more independent . . . to cut the apron strings, so to speak. It's just that now, those reasons don't seem so important anymore."

"Well, the choice is yours, of course. I think running back home would be a mistake, though. The very fact that you're questioning the direction of your life tells me that you're just now ready to break out of the mold that you felt was so stifling in Chicago."

Luke's face broke into a smile. "Leave it to you, to remind me of my own complaints. You're right, of course. I just need to work harder at getting out of my rut. Working with those families in the orchards might just be what I need" His friend drank the last of his coffee, stood, pulled a couple bills from his pocket, and tossed them on the table. "My turn to get the check."

The men parted in the restaurant parking lot after sharing a warm handshake. Luke couldn't wait to get started on his plan. He first stopped at the big discount store in the mall. He wheeled a shopping cart from aisle to aisle, pulling items from the shelves as they caught his eye. The woman at the cash register chuckled as he wrote out a check for his purchases. She had exclaimed over the fact that not many men did their Christmas shopping two months ahead of time. Luke laughed but didn't bother setting her straight. He emptied his purchases into the back of the van and drove to his next stop, a small bookstore near the edge of the city.

"You're mighty chipper this morning, Mr. Forsythe." The clerk greeted him with a smile. "Life must be treating you well."

"If it's not, it's nobody's fault but my own," he answered her cheerfully. He placed a bundle of tracts next to

15

the cash register. They were printed in Spanish. "Have you got any more of these?"

She answered, "No, that's the last of them, but I'm expecting more in any day now."

"Good, I'll check back with you later next week." He accepted his purchase from the clerk and whistling, left the store.

A purpose in life. That's all he needed. To take action. He felt better already. No days and weeks spent planning and plotting. Just jump in and do it!

He drove into his apartment complex intending to check his phone messages in case his parents had called. Opening his mailbox, he was surprised to see a small package among the magazines and envelopes. Turning it over to find a return address, he found none. The postmark showed it had been mailed from the local area however, so sadly, it wouldn't contain any of his mom's homemade fudge.

He cut the tape surrounding the package while he checked his phone messages. No messages. He opened the box. Inside was a pint jar filled with what looked like jam or preserves. A handwritten label adorned the jar which appeared to have come from someone's kitchen. A folded paper was also tucked in the box. He unfolded it, taking note of the colorful hand drawn border.

Dear Mr. Forsythe. Please accept these apricot preserves as a token of my thanks for what you did the other night. That man surely would have been severely injured had you not gone to help. I thought you should be rewarded for your kindness. The note was unsigned.

Luke didn't have to guess who it was from. His mysterious caller. The woman with the intriguing voice. Setting the jar on his kitchen counter he opened it and reached for a spoon. The sweet golden fruit slid onto his tongue like nectar. He rolled it around his mouth, savoring the texture and flavor. Rolling his eyes in pleasure, he recognized that the slight tartness he detected as bits of lemon rind. These were no ordinary preserves. He wondered how she knew that he had a sweet tooth.

He fingered the note again, admiring the detail of the artwork. This was no ordinary woman either. After placing the jar safely into his refrigerator, he pocketed the note and left his apartment.

The drive to the orchards carried none of the anxious questions of the first two trips. The sun shone brightly, adding a flavor of cheerfulness to the crisp fall day. Luke smiled in anticipation, his hands expertly guiding his vehicle along the now familiar road. Barking dogs announced his arrival. The old bus sat in front of the nearest house, a sign of a day off for the workers.

Luke cautiously opened his door, warily watching the dogs for signs of aggressiveness. He spied a man emerging from underneath the bus. He had some kind of tool in his hand and began wiping grease from it with a dirty purple rag. Several dark haired children appeared. The oldest child, a boy about ten years old, grabbed the collar of the largest dog and held it.

"Hi!" Luke grinned widely, extending his hand to the man. The man approached and stood about three feet away making no move to shake Luke's hand. Luke turned his eyes toward the children. They were standing in a circle around the two adults. Their ebony eyes stared at him solemnly. No one spoke.

Luke moved his eyes from child to child, and then back to the man. He swallowed, his throat suddenly dry. He mentally kicked himself for coming so unprepared. At least he should have foreseen this problem and brought a dictionary! "Does anyone here speak English?"

"Si, Senor, we speak English," the man finally answered. "What do you want?"

17

Relief flooded over Luke. Glad the awkward moment was over, he took a deep breath. "I'm looking for a woman."

The man took a menacing step toward him. He lifted his arm as if to strike Luke with the tool he held. His face erupted into a mask of anger and a string of words that Luke couldn't understand spewed from his mouth.

Luke took a step back, realizing his mistake. "Wait. Wait!" He held his arms out in a gesture of peace. "I didn't mean what you think. I meant that I'm looking for a particular woman." He didn't take his eyes off the man whom he had clearly insulted. He took one more step back and shoved his hand into his pocket, pulling out the note that had come with the preserves. "Here," he said, extending the note toward the hostile man. "This woman. The one who did the artwork on this note. Is she here?"

The man looked down at the note, saying nothing. Several children pressed closer, whispering among themselves. A little girl began speaking in Spanish and pointing to the note. Luke couldn't understand what she was saying. She did say one word several times and the other children repeated it. They were all talking at once.

"Angel? Her name is Angel?" He watched as several of the children nodded their heads. Now he was getting somewhere. If he could only talk to the woman. At least *she* was fluent in English and he already had a link with her.

His eyes scanned the nearest row of houses as if expecting her to materialize any moment. "Can you tell me where she lives? Which house is it?" When he looked back at the children, they just looked back with blank expressions on their little faces. He turned to the man again. "Do you know where she lives?"

The man shrugged his shoulders and turned away as if Luke's visit was no longer of any importance.

Luke's feet felt like they were rooted to the ground. At a loss at how to proceed, he was wary of angering the man

18

again. After all, if this group of people were going to be his ministry, he should get off on the right foot with them. It hadn't been the most auspicious beginning.

Suddenly remembering his cargo, he strode to his van and began pulling out the toys he'd purchased that morning. Returning to where the children were gathered, he handed a stack of hand-held electronic games to the oldest boy. The latest and best versions of the games. The ones that the kids at church had been raving about. He eagerly awaited their sounds of joy. Nothing. No joy . . . just looks of puzzlement.

"What do we do with these?" The older boy looked at Luke with accusing eyes. "We have no batteries for playing these games."

Luke groaned. So much for making friends. He was doing everything wrong. He walked back to the van, looking for anything that would be suitable for the little group. One toy dump truck and a teddy bear. He hesitantly offered them. A small girl stepped forward and clasped the brown fuzzy bear to her chest. She raised her beautiful dark eyes and favored Luke with a shy smile.

"Maria, tell the man thank you," the oldest boy sternly said, pushing her slightly forward.

She barely whispered the words, but Luke felt ten feet tall. He placed the truck on the ground, not wanting to select one child over another. Then he passed out the gospel tracts that were written in Spanish. Promising to bring batteries next time, and wanting to leave on a high note, he climbed into his van to leave. As he drove away, he looked into his rear-view mirror and could see the tracts blowing in the wind, adding patches of brightly colored splotches on the brown and barren ground.

***

Her father's voice thundered, breaking through the fog of Aimee's sleep. *"You have sinned! You've broken one of God's Commandments! It's only right that you pay!"*

19

She fought her way out of the nightmare, tears streaming down her face. Untangling herself from the damp quilt, drenched in sweat, she reached for the switch on the bedside lamp. A soft glow flooded the tiny bedroom, chasing away the angry words. Aimee knew what to do. This wasn't the first time her sleep had been interrupted by her father's wrath. The accusation filled dreams had been part of her life for so long that she couldn't remember when they weren't intertwined with each night's slumber. Except recently. In fact, she realized, she hadn't had a nightmare in months. Why would they come back now, of all times? Just when she was finally getting her life together?

The light helped. She opened the window shade and sunlight poured in. Aimee guessed it was nearly noon. Sleeping late had become a habit. The fact that other people had been up and about for hours didn't bother her. They didn't have anything to do with her. She had worked all night again. The peace and quiet of the darkness helped her concentrate while she created. But now, she felt anything but peaceful. The familiar nightmare had shaken her.

Aimee wondered if her father ever thought about her . . . if he still hated her. She missed him, but not enough to go home. It wasn't even her home anymore. He'd made that plain. She had her own home now. Soon she would begin her life. A life like everyone else had. But first she had to earn enough money to erase the scars of the past. The scar. She touched her cheek and followed the path of the ugly red welt with her fingers. It zigzagged from just below her eye to her jawbone, twisting her face into a hideous remembrance reaching into her very soul. Fresh tears welled up in her eyes. She didn't need this reminder of her mother's death. She would never forget as long as she lived.

Aimee picked up the phone. She would call Mrs. Crow. While she wouldn't confide in the woman, her friend and editor would at least help drive away the sound of her father's voice. The phone on the other end of the line rang and rang. Disappointed, Aimee set the receiver in its cradle.

Realizing it was Saturday and the office was probably closed, she paced aimlessly around the room, wishing she knew Mrs. Crow's home number. There wasn't anyone else to call. True, her isolation was one of her own making, but she couldn't stand the pitying looks, inevitable questions and denouncements. There were times like this, though, that she would have welcomed the voice of even a stranger.

Her father's words wouldn't go away. She pressed her hands against her temples, her head pounding. Looking around the room, she sought anything that would provide some distraction. A cup of tea might help, she thought, and set about filling the teakettle. It dropped from her hand, spilling water on the floor. She pulled a terry cloth towel from the drawer and dropped it on the spilled water. Stepping over the mess, she made her way back to the phone. Her eyes lit on the newspaper picture she had taped above her computer.

Maybe she could call and see if he received the preserves. Taking a deep breath, she looked up the number and dialed. What would she say if he answered? She should have thought this out more carefully.

"Hello?"

"Mr. Forsythe?"

"Speaking."

"Mr. Forsythe, I am calling to see if you received the apricot preserves I sent."

"Angel!" It sounded like to Aimee that Luke almost shouted the name out in gladness. "I've been hoping you'd call."

He must think I'm someone else. "Angel? This isn't Angel."

"But I thought . . . Angel isn't your name?"

Aimee hesitated. She had to keep a distance from this man. If he found out her name, he could find out where she lived. And maybe even the other things. She had to think of a way to keep her anonymity and still keep the conversation going. Already the darkness of her nightmare was dwindling. If she could just keep him talking, it would go away completely. "I meant . . . hardly anyone calls me by that name."

"Well," she could almost picture him smiling as he continued, "a very pretty little girl named Maria must be one of those that do."

"Maria? You spoke with her?"

"We didn't exactly talk . . . but I did meet her. She's a little shy, isn't she?"

Leaning back in her chair, Aimee could feel her shoulders start to relax. She was glad she had called him. His voice reverberated with friendliness.

"Angel?"

"What? Oh. Yes, all of the children at the orchards are shy around strangers. They're very sweet when you get to know them, though."

"Have you known them long?"

"About three years now, I think. Right after I first moved here."

"Do you live near them?"

Aimee sat upright in her chair. He was asking questions. If she could only keep him talking to her without him asking so many questions. "No. Not near them. I do go visit them once in a while, though."

"Maybe I'll see you there sometime. I plan on spending quite a bit of time there."

"Whatever for?"

"I'd like to see if there's anything I can do to help them. They sure look like they could use some help. This is why I told you I was glad you'd called. I was hoping you could fill me in on what their needs might be."

"I don't think they welcome outsiders. People haven't been very friendly to them."

"All the more reason for me to go. Look . . . could we meet for coffee or something and you could tell me some more? I'm really anxious to get started."

"No!" Aimee looked at Luke's picture on her wall, wishing she *could* meet him for coffee. He'd probably stalk away in disgust as soon as he saw her face, though. No. She would handle this by telephone.

"Did I say something wrong?"

"I meant . . . I'm sorry. I didn't mean to be abrupt. It's just that I'm working on a deadline right now and can't get away."

"Oh. Could I call you then?"

Aimee weighed his request. If she gave him her phone number, would he be able to find her? Would he show up on her doorstep? She didn't know. Better to be safe. "I'm really pretty busy. Would it be all right if I called you instead, Mr. Forsythe?"

"Sure . . . anytime. And my name's Luke."

Luke! He expected her to call him by his first name. As if they were already friends. Aimee had reservations about her ability to make and keep a friend. However, she was determined that her entire life wasn't going to be devoid of such social pleasures. This is what she had been working toward all along wasn't it? "I'm not sure how I could be of help . . . but perhaps I could answer any questions you may have."

"This is great, Angel. I have tons of questions for you. For starters, do the families at the end of the road live there year around?"

His enthusiasm intrigued her. Although she'd figured out he was an upbeat person from reading his column, it still took her by surprise. Maybe it was his deep baritone voice coming over the phone line that seemed to fill her gloomy room with sunshine. Maybe it was just the stark contrast between Luke's voice and the harsh voice of her father. Whatever the reason, she felt drawn into his fervor. "Yes, for the most part, the families you saw live there all year. They have other relatives and friends that come here from Mexico who work during the harvest and then go home again. But Juan and his family have been there as long as I've known them."

"Juan?"

"The man whom you saved from the beating last week. He's Maria and Gabe's father."

"Is Gabe about ten years old? And kind of skinny?"

"That sounds like him. Why are you so interested in these people? Are you going to write about them in your paper?"

She heard him chuckle and say, "I thought my motives would be obvious to an angel such as you."

Aimee sucked in her breath, stunned by his words. Mr. Luke Forsythe certainly had a mistaken impression of her. Maybe she should tell him the truth now before he wasted any more of his time with her. Her desire to keep hearing his voice, however, squelched that idea. "I'm *no* angel. But if I were, there's much I would do for those families."

"There's much I would like to do as well, with your help and God's."

"God's?"

"Yes. God loves them and I want to tell them about it. You know . . . to have them experience that love firsthand?"

"You talk like God's a personal friend of yours." Aimee felt her jaw tighten. Was there no place she could hide from God? His name cropped up in every nightmare and now this? She sensed she'd offended the man on the other end of the line. No doubt he picked up on the sarcastic tone in her voice. She couldn't bring herself to apologize, though. The

God she knew who demanded retribution at every turn would probably strike her dead for lying.

"I doubt if those families care much for religion. They have their hands full just keeping food on the table."

"Maybe they deserve the opportunity to choose for themselves."

"We each make our own opportunities, Mr. Forsythe. The people at the orchards are working very hard to make a life for their children. Better than they had as children. We could more effectively help them if we didn't try to force our version of religion down their throats. They need respect and a life free of the kind of bigoted persecution that seems prevalent around here."

"I can see you have strong opinions, Angel. All I can tell you is that I sincerely want to do what I can to help them. I'll need your advice though. And please, won't you call me Luke?"

Aimee considered his words. Wasn't he just trying to do what she had been doing for the last couple of years? He might even be able to intervene in the problems they were having up there. Obviously the violence was escalating and there was nothing she could do to stop it.

Would Luke's God finally stop punishing her if she agreed to help? Would anything she did ever make up for the wrong she had committed? She hoped so. All she had to do was find the magic key to God's forgiveness. Maybe if God forgave her, her father would, too. Or maybe she was chasing rainbows and was already irretrievably condemned. She had to try. As long as she was alive, there had to be a chance for her.

She gazed at his picture again, trying to measure his sincerity. "I'll do what I can, Mr . . . . Luke."

"You won't be sorry. I promise." His voice sounded as soothing as a soft breeze on a summer's day. "I know this maybe an imposition, seeing how busy you are, but if you

25

could just stay in touch with me. You know . . . just in case I have any questions or problems communicating with these people."

"I guess I could call you sometimes."

"Let me give you my office number. Do you have a pencil?"

"Yes. Go ahead." Aimee wrote the phone number on a pad next to his home number. Then she picked up a colored pen and doodled scrolls around both numbers.

"Could you tell me how many folks are living up there right now?"

"Let me think. Six families altogether. Counting the children and grandparents, between twenty-five and thirty people, I would guess." She realized that she herself had not seen all of them at one time. Mostly just the children. Most of them had not seen her either. Luke probably thought she was a regular visitor to their homes. It didn't matter. He could think what he liked. They could still help each other. She would just make sure that they never crossed paths.

"Angel, I'm really glad you called. And thank you for the preserves. I liked them very much. Please call me again soon."

"I will. Goodbye, Luke."

"Goodbye."

Aimee gently hung up her phone. She was glad she'd called him. Her nightmare and resultant headache were now just dim memories. She wished his picture in the newspaper was in color so she could see the color of his eyes. The black and white photo made them look light colored . . . blue or even hazel. He had such a nice voice. Maybe she would see him and talk to him in person someday. It wouldn't happen soon, but some day in the future.

She mentally calculated how long it would be before she would be ready to face the world. Maybe a year from now, or even a little longer. She had been saving for the surgery for a long time now. Even before she had left her father's house, she had been putting aside pennies for this. Her father said she was vain and sinful . . . That it was God's will that she bear the scar. Aimee hoped that God had punished her long enough.

CHAPTER THREE

The noise level in the church sanctuary rose as the members of the congregation gathered their coats, purses, and children to go home for their Sunday dinners. Luke put his hymnal away and turned to the young couple standing next to him. He had met them soon after joining the church and had immediately liked them. Mitch helped his young wife with her coat. Luke admired the way they related to each other, always affectionate and respectful. They'd been married for several years but, much to their disappointment had no children. Carrie worked as a nurse in a large local hospital and Mitch was an attorney. From all outward appearances, they were doing well financially.

"Mitch, I noticed you driving a new SUV this morning."

His friend smiled and said, "Yep. We just picked it up last week. I thought Carrie should have something that would handle well in the snow." He threw his arm around his wife's shoulders and gave her a quick peck on her forehead. She blushed, and then greeted Luke with her usual friendly smile.

"How many people will it hold?"

"Why don't you walk out with us, and take a look, Luke? Thinking about buying one yourself?"

"Nah, I'm pretty happy with my van. However, I'd like to press you into service if you'd be interested."

The threesome left the church together, and Luke outlined his plan as they strolled to the parking lot. He'd already found a few other people who had agreed to drive their cars to the orchards the following Sunday. If Mitch and Carrie could come too, he was sure there would be enough vehicles to provide transportation for anyone who would like to come to church. He'd ask Angel if she'd like to come along, too. The people at the orchards would probably appreciate having a familiar face along.

Mitch and Carrie agreed to help and Luke's thoughts turned to Angel as he climbed into his own van. She'd seemed somewhat reticent the day before, but after all, she really didn't know him from Adam. He was sure that she'd come around as soon as she got to know him better. He hoped she'd call him again soon. He liked the sound of her voice and wondered what she looked like.   She's probably a wrinkled old woman, old enough to be his grandmother. He chuckled aloud at the thought. His grandmother had never made him anticipate *her* calls like Angel did. What was it about her? The voice, surely. But there was something else about her. Her shyness? He'd never been attracted to shy women before.

Angel was different. He sensed she was special. She was also troubled. That reference she made about religion sounded like she was put off by it. What a disappointment it would be if he had finally found a woman with a voice like an angel, looked like a model . . . which he was now convinced she must, and then didn't share his beliefs.

Luke pulled up to the window of a fast food restaurant and ordered two hamburgers and fries. The nip in the air outside stung his face, but he still opted for a large chocolate shake rather than a cup of hot coffee that the anonymous voice from the speaker suggested. Another solitary meal. He could've taken Mitch and Carrie up on their invitation to eat with them, but he was anxious to visit the orchards again.

Snow, mixed with rain, hit his windshield as he left the city of Wenatchee behind. The weather in eastern Washington wasn't much different from Chicago. The terrain however was totally dissimilar. Luke preferred the mountains and canyons near Wenatchee to the flatness of his home in Illinois. He reflected on the times he could look out of his father's sixth floor office window and see the

Sears Tower twenty miles away. Here, each bend in the road offered a new view. Entire communities were hidden away in the foothills of the Cascades. At that moment, a turn in the highway revealed the broad Columbia River. It must have been a sight to see before the numerous dams were built and it was still free flowing. The hills rose sharply to his left and he slowed to turn onto the road that would lead him to the orchards.

The orchards were at least five miles from the main highway. Icy sleet finally made it necessary for Luke turn on his wipers. Even though it was midday, the darkness of the impending storm made visibility poor. He almost missed the gravel road turnoff. The same two barking dogs announced his arrival. He wondered if he should have brought cheeseburgers for the dogs that weren't much friendlier than their owners.

Luke parked directly in front of the first house. A movement of a blanket draped across a window, let him know that the canine alarms had indeed announced his arrival to the people inside. The door opened, and Gabe, the boy he had met before, stepped out onto the wooden porch.

Luke cautiously opened his door, keeping his eye on the snarling dogs. As before, the boy advanced and restrained the biggest one.

"Hi."

Gabe half acknowledged his greeting, but didn't smile in return. Luke wished again that Angel was available to act as a mediator. He bet that they would be happier to see her than they were him.

"Are your parents at home?"

The boy led the growling dog to a chain that was attached to an outside faucet. He hooked the chain to the dog's collar and motioned for Luke to follow him. Gabe opened the door and disappeared inside the house.

30

Luke hesitated at the door, listening to the noise of a radio that drowned out what the boy was saying. Luke could hear that it was a Spanish radio station and was surprised. He didn't know one existed in the area. A man Luke assumed was Gabe's father appeared in the doorway.

"Juan?" Luke stuck out his hand in greeting to the other man. He looked familiar. It suddenly dawned on him, when he saw a cut over the man's eye, that this was the man who had been the beating victim.

"Si. Who are you?" Juan hesitantly offered his hand in return, but removed it immediately after a polite, but cool grasp.

Luke didn't see any reason to remind the other man of the altercation. He would probably seem to be butting in where he didn't belong. "I'm Luke Forsythe. I was here yesterday to bring toys for the children. I've brought the batteries for the toys and I'd like to visit with you for a few minutes if I could."

Juan looked at Luke suspiciously. His eyes flicked from his uninvited visitor to the shiny van outside. "Are you from the school?"

"No. I'm just a friend. A friend of Angel's, actually." Luke realized that he was stretching the truth and again wished that Angel had come with him. This wasn't the biggest welcome he had ever received. He struggled for words which might form a common ground between the two men.

Just then, little Maria poked her head around the door. She held the teddy bear in her arms. Her father protectively drew her close to him and listened as she spoke to him in soft Spanish phrases.

Juan's face softened somewhat. "Come in. It is cold outside." He led the way into the small living room. Gesturing to a chair, he walked to the door of the adjoining kitchenette and said something to the woman standing at the stove. Wiping her hands on her apron, she turned and favored Luke with the same shy smile that graced her daughter's face.

"Hi. My name is Luke." He stood and put out his hand, feeling for the first time that he was truly welcome.

"My name is Carmelita and this is my husband, Juan. You've already met our children."

Luke shifted his weight from leg to leg, unsure how he should proceed. "Yes I have. You have a very nice family." He watched Carmelita's face light up with pride. Their home may have been lacking in modern conveniences, but the little family displayed a closeness many wealthy people would envy.

"Would you like to eat with us? I am making tortillas."

Her invitation seemed as sincere as her smile. Luke didn't want to offend her but even his large appetite couldn't accommodate another bite of food after what he's just eaten. The aroma coming from the kitchen was inviting though, and he was tempted to take a chance. "I'd love to, but I just ate a big meal before coming here. It does smell good, though. Perhaps you'd invite me again."

Carmelita looked disappointed, but Juan just shrugged. They all stood awkwardly for a few moments before Luke finally announced the reason for his visit.

"I noticed the families here don't have much in the way of reliable transportation. My friends and I would like to come here next Sunday morning and take everyone to church and Sunday school. The little ones will enjoy the music and stories."

"And the parents? What would the parents enjoy about your church?"

Luke looked at Juan, surprised at the bitterness in the other man's voice. This was the second time he had heard that tone from someone when he mentioned God or church. The first was from Angel and he was at a loss on how to understand it. Evidently both Angel and Juan had some reason to feel the way they did. He wished he knew how to assure them of God's love. The only way he knew how was to show them his own caring. Were there many people like this? Had he spent so much time in his own little world that he had failed to notice?

"The adults enjoy the same things, Juan. The music. The Bible stories. And of course the fellowship."

Juan didn't seem to be easily convinced. "How many Latinos are there in this church of yours to *fellowship* with?" His voice was laced with sarcasm.

"Why . . . I admit, I don't know, Juan. I'm sure there are a few, though." *Oh man. I'm just making things worse and worse. Why did I ever think I could make a difference?* "Juan, I can assure you that you and your family and all the rest of these folks will be made welcome. I'll be here next Sunday morning at nine to drive whoever wants to go."

He took a step toward the door, feeling like his smile was pasted on his face. The two children were silent during their father's conversation. Carmelita looked slightly embarrassed but said nothing either. Juan took a step toward the door as well and Luke knew it was time to leave.

"Oh. Here are those batteries for the kid's games." He thrust the package toward Juan. "Thank you for the dinner invitation, Carmelita. I'm looking forward to trying your delicious smelling cooking someday. I'll see everyone next week." He stepped through the door Juan hastily opened for him. The big dog jumped to its feet and growled, making Luke feel even more unwelcome. After the pleasant warmth of the little house, the cold wind and rain stung his eyes as he retreated to his van. He knew one thing, though . . . he was nowhere near ready to throw in the towel. *What had caused these people to be so untrusting?*

As he slowly drove down the hill, Luke turned on the heater, not waiting for the defogger to clear his windows.

The wipers turned to the fastest setting adding a comforting clunking to the driving sleet outside. Stopping at the first stop sign, he noticed a sheriff's vehicle parked on the shoulder. He signaled to turn and pulled onto the paved road. A flashing blue light appeared immediately in his rear-view mirror. *Oh great. Just what I needed.*

Pulling onto the shoulder, he wondered what he had done wrong. Did everyone feel the same anxiousness that he did during a stop like this? Expecting a verbal warning for some minor infraction, he was taken back by the sound of a flashlight hitting the glass next to his ear. He quickly lowered the window.

"What's wrong, officer?"

"Let me see your license and registration." The voice was gruff, unfriendly, and familiar.

Luke handed over the documents to the same deputy he'd seen the night the Juan had been beaten. He waited for what seemed like forever while the uniformed grouch sat in the patrol car, presumably checking to see if Luke was a wanted felon. Luke considered himself a responsible and careful driver and was irritated at the other man's treatment of him. He spotted the officer returning and again opened his window, only to be slapped in the face with a wet wind gust. Luke tried to arrange his face in to a pleasant look.

The cop spoke in clipped hard tones. "You were up here the other night."

"Yes, sir. I thought I'd explained . . ."

"What brings you up here again?"

"I'm visiting friends."

"I don't recall anyone saying they were friends with a newspaperman."

"Look, I'm not aware that I was doing anything wrong. If you're going to write me a ticket, I'd like to know . . ."

"Don't give me any lip. I don't need a reason to check out suspicious persons."

34

Suspicious persons? Luke couldn't believe his ears. He just wanted to get away from here and spend the rest of the day in front of the tube watching football.

"Step out of the car."

"What?" Luke's stomach tightened.

The deputy wrenched open Luke's door and put his pudgy fingers around the Luke's wrist. "I said, step out of the car."

Luke complied immediately, his annoyance turning to anxiety. What was this all about? He obediently turned as directed and placed his hands on the hood. Never had he felt as violated as when he felt the deputy pat down his chest, back and legs. *So this is what it's like to be frisked.* He nearly stumbled when the other man swung him back around to face him.

"Okay, you can go. But I'm warning you . . . I don't want to see you hanging around here again." The deputy's face was so close to Luke's that he could smell stale cigars. He gave Luke an almost imperceptible shove and swaggered back to his patrol car.

Luke stood next to his van, soaking wet and cold, and watched the deputy drive off. He had been so stunned by the whole episode he hadn't even taken note of the man's nametag. He would never forget his face, though. Perplexed didn't even begin to describe his feelings as he climbed back in the van. Anger had taken over. An anger as foreign to Luke as the experience with the cop. He silently petitioned God for and wisdom and peace as he drove home.

***

Aimee saw the whole thing from her hiding place behind the trees. Glimpsing Luke's van go up the hill earlier, had prompted her to put on her hat and coat and wait near the road for him to return. She knew it was his van. She had memorized every feature of it the first night she had called him. Today she had only meant to stand under the

35

protective branches long enough to catch a peek at him when he drove by.

Then that cop had shown up. He'd followed Luke almost to the top of the hill and turned around and waited for him just as she had. Her fear had made her cringe further into the shielding evergreen foliage.

Luke's calm demeanor during his humiliating treatment by the deputy filled Aimee with admiration. He must have been furious, but had exhibited such self-control. Aimee knew what the deputy was up to. Now maybe Luke did, too. Maybe he could put a stop to it. No one else was going to, that's for sure. It had been going on way too long. *But Luke is smart. He'll be able to figure out how to stop it.*

Even from her hidden vantage point, Aimee could see that Luke was every bit as handsome in person as he was in the newspaper photo. The rain had plastered his wind breaker to his chest, revealing a well-kept body, unadorned by fat. He was tall, too. A few inches taller than herself, she guessed.

If only she could meet him in person someday. But she would. Just not right away. After her surgery. Would he think she was pretty then? Her mother had always told her how pretty she was. But mothers always think that, don't they? Still, if one only looked at the good half of her face, they wouldn't see a reason to cringe.

She watched him drive out of sight. He had a nice van. It looked rather new but was more of a family car than something sporty she imagined a bachelor would drive. Could he be married? She would have to find out before she spent any more time mooning over him. But how? Just come out and ask him? Well, there was no hurry, really. Besides, if he weren't married, he probably had a steady girlfriend. Or lots of girlfriends. Aimee smiled, happiness a rare occurrence these days. Just imagining the possibility of being one of Luke's girlfriends brought a little happiness to her heart.

***

Luke ground his teeth in anger. His hand tightly gripped the phone back at his apartment, as he recounted his experience with the deputy to his friend Mitch.

"Are you sure that you weren't speeding, or had a burnt out tail light or anything like that?"

"No, Mitch. It's just like I told you. There was nothing wrong at all. I've got to believe that if there were, Officer Friendly would have given me a ticket. He acted like he was just waiting for any excuse."

"Well, I wasn't there, but based on your description, I'd say that this was an illegal stop. The police can't pull you over unless you've committed a violation. Or, of course, unless you've got stolen plates on your car or something like that."

Luke felt better, now that his friend had supported his own beliefs. "So what can I do? Should I lodge a complaint?"

"I don't think it would do much good, Luke. The guy was probably just having a bad day. You said that he didn't actually assault you. Besides, there were no witnesses. It would be just your word against his. You know, the sheriff probably won't take your word against that of one of his own men."

"That doesn't seem right. People shouldn't have to be treated like that. If he treated me like that, I wonder how he treats minorities . . ., which brings me to my next question. Can he tell me to stay away from the orchards?"

"I don't see how he can. If you are an invited guest, it's nobody's business but yours. The only thing he could remotely accuse you of is trespassing. And then, that's only if someone, the owner of the property, for instance, files a complaint against you."

37

"So it sounds like you think I should just blow it off, huh?"

"I would, Luke. I'm not saying that the cop was acting appropriately. It's just that unless you can prove he caused you some damage, there's not much point in pursuing it."

"Well, thanks anyway, Mitch. Sorry to interrupt the football game."

"No problem, buddy. Anytime. See you next week."

"Okay, goodbye." Luke hung up. He picked up his remote control and pressed the mute button, allowing the noise of the Seahawk's game to fill his apartment. They were behind, too far behind to catch up in the fourth quarter. What a day this had turned out to be. Luke recalled the senior pastor speaking so eloquently that morning about counting your blessings. Perhaps he should have listened more closely. Blessings were in short supply today. When had he become such a grouch?

He flipped through the channels, looking for anything to help pass the time. Reruns, cartoons, and a shopping channel. An unseen salesperson raved about the attributes of gold jewelry. A little counter displayed at the bottom of the screen told the viewers that forty people per minute were purchasing the advertised necklaces for their loved ones. Does every guy in the country have someone special to buy for? From all appearances, they did.

He flipped to another channel He bet that very few men his age were spending Sunday afternoon alone. That's probably why the tavern parking lots were always full. The people inside merely want to spend their day off in a crowd of friendly faces. Okay, blessing number one. He attended a Bible teaching church with hundreds of friendly faces all around him.

Luke switched channels again. This time the announcer was extolling the virtues of a romantic Bed and Breakfast not too far from Wenatchee. A perfect honeymoon or

38

anniversary destination, he was saying. The camera panned over an antique filled room that opened onto its own private deck. Steam rose from a hot tub, conjuring up images of a romantic moment between two lovers. The lit fireplace added just the right cozy touch to the picture. An idea suddenly occurred to Luke. What a great gift for his parents! He couldn't remember when they last had a vacation that wasn't an add-on to one of his dad's business trips. He could invite them out here and book one of those rooms for them for an entire weekend. He reached for his phone. His mother's familiar voice answered on the third ring.

"Hello, Mom."

"Lukie. I'm glad you called. How are you?"

"I'm just fine. How is Dad?"

"Oh, honey, the medicine isn't helping as much as we'd hoped. He's having chest pains again."

"Mom, why didn't you call me?"

"Honey, I didn't want to worry you. Besides, we don't know what we're going to do yet."

"Can't they give him something stronger?"

"No. The nitroglycerin is really only masking the real problem. Your Dad is going in for an angiogram tomorrow. The doctors will know more then."

"Do you want me to come home?"

"No. That's not necessary. It's just a test. I'll let you know as soon as we know anything. Your Dad's taking a nap right now. He's going to be sorry he missed your call. I don't want to wake him, though. He needs his rest."

"That's all right, Mom. Just give him my love. And please call me tomorrow. You've got my work number?"

"I have both your numbers written here and in my purse. I'll call you, honey."

"Thanks, Mom. Take care. I love you."

"We love you too, Lukie."

Luke didn't waste anytime after the phone call. He dropped to his knees next to the couch and prayed for his dad's health. "And Lord, please give Mom the strength she needs. I don't know what she would do if she were to lose Dad." Unfamiliar tears burned Luke's eyes as he contemplated the thought of his mother waiting alone at the hospital for word from the doctors. "And Lord, thank you for all the blessings you've heaped on me and my family for all these years. As your child and humble servant, I ask that you use me to be a blessing to others. Protect the orchard families from harm and please open their hearts so that I may share Your love with them. Bless Angel, and if You could, please send someone to her with Your message of love as well."

Luke stayed on his knees after he had finished his requests, thanking God for the answers and for the peace that filled him.

CHAPTER FOUR

Aimee looked at her kitchen clock for the fourth time. *What time does he get to work? If I call and he's not there yet, someone will only ask me to leave my number.* She paced to her desk and back to the kitchen.

Nine o'clock. Surely he'd be in his office. She dialed the number for the newspaper she'd written down before and asked for Luke.

"Hello?"

"I saw what that deputy did to you."

"Angel?"

"Huh?"

"Is this Angel from the orchards? I know your voice."

It wouldn't hurt to give him my first name. That's better than lying about it. "My name isn't actually Angel. I'm sorry I left you with that impression. Sometimes the children call me that, but my name is really Aimee."

"Oh. And what is your last name?"

"I called to talk to you about that deputy. I saw what happened." Aimee waited for Luke to break the long silence on the other end of the line. "Are you still there?"

"Yes. Look. Would you like to get together for lunch and discuss this?"

Aimee wanted nothing better than to spend time with Luke. But that would have to wait for a future time . . . when she was healed and normal again. If Luke saw her the way she was, he'd cringe in disgust. And that would be before he would even know what the damage represented.

"That wouldn't be possible. I have to work. I have deadlines to meet."

"What kind of work do you do?"

He seems so interested in me? Like he really wants to be my friend. "Oh, only a little freelancing."

"Another writer? Like me?"

"Not exactly. I can't talk long. What did that deputy say to you?"

"He did his best to warn me away from the orchards. Do you know of any reason he'd do this?"

Did she dare tell him? She trusted him, but after seeing the deputy try and scare him off, would he be safe if he knew the whole truth? "He doesn't like strangers. Maybe he's afraid you'll stir up trouble."

"What kind of fuss could I possibly stir up? If he wasn't a member of the law, I'd think he was hiding something. He seems to know I work for a newspaper. Does he live nearby? Does he have family up there?"

"No. He has no one there. And I don't know where he lives." Aimee's concern for the families on the hill outweighed her worry about Luke's safety. She'd have to tell him everything she knew. "I think he's taking money from them. Juan must have tried to fight back and that's why he got beat up that first night."

Luke let out a long, low whistle. "I had no idea. The deputy is the one who inflicted those bruises on Juan? So this is why you didn't call the police that night?"

"Yes. I don't know if they would have stopped it."

"We have to report this!"

"It wouldn't do any good. It's our word against his. The families are too afraid to say anything."

"Can we get proof? Can't we encourage them to confide in us?"

"They have too much to lose. They're afraid they could lose their work permits or Green Cards. These jobs mean their families here and back at home won't starve."

Luke ran his fingers through his hair. *Lord, I thought you wanted me to bring those people to church. I don't know if I'm up to taking on the problem Aimee is sharing. At least not on my own. What do you want me to do?*

42

"Luke? Can you help? Do you know anyone who could look into the problem?"

"Let me think. One of the problems is their isolation from the rest of the community. The more people aware of them, the less chance anyone can take advantage of them. As far as that deputy goes, let me ask around. If he's extorting money, there has to be some evidence somewhere. Maybe he's done something like this in the past."

"You've got to be careful. Promise me. If anyone finds out you're checking around, things could get a lot worse."

Aimee's tone again reminded him of the passion for the families she exhibited the first night she'd called him. How many women would bother to try and help those less fortunate then themselves?

"I'll be careful. Let me have your phone number so we can keep in touch."

"It's better if I call you."

One of the secretaries motioned to him before he had a chance to try and persuade her to give him the number.

"Aimee, I have another call coming in. Will you promise to call me back?"

"I promise. And Luke?"

"Yes?"

"Thank you so much for caring. Goodbye." The line went dead.

Luke picked up the other line. "Lukie?"

"Mom!"

"I'm at the hospital. Your dad has some blockages in his heart. They're going to do an angioplasty."

Luke wasn't sure what that entailed, but it sounded serious and his mother sounded scared. "Mom, I can be out on the next plane."

"You wouldn't get here in time. They're taking him in to surgery right now. I only wanted to let you know so you could pray for him." Her voice broke. "I'll call you as soon as I hear anything more."

"Let's pray right now." With his mother still on the line, Luke prayed . . . first for his father, and then for the doctors and surgical team. "*And bless Aimee*," he whispered.

Hanging up the phone, he glanced up to see Partlow standing in front of his desk. "I want a word with you. In my office. Now. He turned and strode off.

Luke followed, puzzled about his boss's angry demeanor. Had he heard him praying and objected? When they reached the office, Partlow closed the door and gestured for Luke to sit down.

"How's your column going?"

Not sure what to answer, Luke responded, Fine." Since it hadn't been long sine they'd last talked, the underlying reason for that meeting remained unclear.

"Are you happy here?" Partlow's tone of voice did not suggest a promotion was in the offing. The question was laced with innuendo.

"Like I said the other day, I like my job, but I'd like to try my hand at some more serious pieces."

"And if I recall correctly, I told you this paper is not interested in any stories about immigrants."

"I've been thinking lately about a series of interest to the general public."

"And that would be?"

"Police brutality. Or corruption. What do you think?"

"I think," his boss stretched out the word, "You are looking for trouble."

"What do you mean?"

"I mean, let the larger, big city newspaper delve into those issues. This isn't what my paper is about."

"But your paper reports crime."

Yes, but that is a matter of public record. We're not about to begin slinging false accusations around about the men and women who lay their lives on the line for us everyday." Partlow's face turned a shade of deep red.

Luke couldn't help wondering what had brought that remark on. "I'm not suggesting we print any libelous statements. I only think it's something I'd like to look into."

Partlow fixed him with a stare, that had it been a sword, would have impaled Luke to the wall. "And you think you already have the start to such a story? That one of our fine officers might be involved in any such thing?"

Luke thought for a moment. Why was Partlow being so defensive? Had that deputy complained about his visit to the orchards? That might explain his boss's reluctance to touch that story as well. That had to be it. Something stinky was going on.

"Sir, are you indicating you want me to stick to *fluff* pieces?

"I'm telling you, for the second time, by the way, I am quite satisfied with the work you are currently doing. Perhaps in the future, I'll send you out on a few assignments . . . after you've proven you understand the mission of this paper."

Luke didn't need a baseball bat to hit him in the head. Partlow had given him notice.

"If you find you would prefer working for another paper, I'll be happy to write you a reference."

Yep. I've been told what my boundaries are. Luke stood and put out his hand. "Thank you for explaining your concerns, sir. I won't bother you with anymore ideas which don't fit in with this paper."

Partlow shook Luke's hand and patted him on the shoulder, all the while leading him to the door. "I expect to hear many more good reports about your column, son. Keep up the good work."

Luke found himself standing outside the door with the click of the door lock still echoing in his ears. He glanced at

45

the phone on Partlow's secretary's desk. A light went on, indicating his boss was making a call. He'd give a month's salary to know who he was calling.

***

Aimee thought back to the phone conversation with Luke. Now that he had agreed to help, she was anxious to get started. She couldn't get the orchard families out of her mind. She tried to put the subject aside and work on the batch of greeting cards Mrs. Crow expected. However, the children's faces intruded themselves into every verse.

Aimee gave up and made several sketches of black-haired children with rosy lips and dark eyes. Children laughing, playing, singing and even some with pensive little faces. Her hands moved swiftly, only stopping to pick up different colored pens. Hours passed, and Aimee was finally forced to stop when her stomach protested the lack of food.

After a brief break, when she ate a sandwich and brewed a fresh pot of tea, she reviewed what she'd done. The children showed color, life, and a poignancy lacking in her prior work.

Would Mrs. Crow be as taken with images of these children as she was? Aimee knew this batch of cards represented love, where the ones before only showed her drawing skills.

Maybe she'd go up the hill and speak to the children before the men and older boys came home from work. She might be able to get some information from them about the deputy. They might know how often he came. How long he stayed. Unfortunately, only the very young children would be at home.

It made her ill to hear of mere children working at jobs which should be reserved for men. She knew by law, the children had to be at least twelve years old to work, but suspected some lied about their ages in order to help earn money for their families.

46

The few women who stayed behind to care for the littlest children and babies would not be forthcoming with information about the deputy. They might even take exception to her bringing up the subject with the children. Their community's sense of pride requires they handle their own problems. Besides, Aimee didn't want to do anything which might bring any danger to them. She'd have to be careful.

Aimee decided to take the car out and go to the grocery store before visiting the orchards. A little candy would go a long way to encourage the children to gather around. She also wanted to stock up on her own food supplies before any winter snowstorms hit. The county couldn't always sand every road in a timely matter, and the drive up the hill could be treacherous.

She gathered up her drawings and placed them in a mailing envelope for Mrs. Crow. The post office was near the grocery store and she could mail it and pick up some more priority envelopes and stamps while there.

Aimee bundled up for the drive. The heater in the old car only worked once in a while. The cost of repairing it would probably exceed the value of the vehicle, so she didn't bother. As long as it got her back and forth, that's all that mattered.

She quickly finished her errands, returned home and put away her groceries. Then she got on her bike and headed up the hill with candy for the children. Fruit would have been better for them, but they had plenty of culls from the orchards so this would be a special treat. She'd also managed to get the butcher at the grocery to give her some bones for the dogs.

The ride gave her a chance to think about Luke again. How she envied other women who didn't have to hide behind their front doors. A normal woman would have jumped at the chance to have lunch with a man like him. He was smart, handsome, and best of all, he really cared about others. Even his references to God were nothing like the religion her father subscribed to.

Amy wondered how long it would be before she could reveal herself to him. Even after her surgery, it would take some time for the scars to heal. Would he still be around? And willing to take her to lunch then? Or will another woman have gotten him to the altar by then?

Somewhat out of breath from the climb, she finally arrived at the row of dilapidated houses. The children, followed by a couple of their dogs, ran to her, shouting and laughing. Aimee noticed a couple of them had bare feet, even though the temperature hovered just above freezing. She was sure their little toes must be blue under the layers of dust and dirt.

Their lack of footwear probably had more to do with scant money rather than neglect. They needed to dress their children who went to school first. Then they bought food. The free lunches at school helped a lot, but there wasn't money left over for any luxuries, let alone all the necessaries.

Aimee's fury at the deputy emerged every time she visited there. How dare he take advantage of these people! He had to be stopped.

Aimee hugged little Maria, her love for the child pushing out thoughts of the evil in the world. Maria had a brand new teddy bear in her arms. "Where did you get this?"

"The nice man brought it. He brought some other things too."

Surely she doesn't mean the deputy. Who else had been here? Luke! A rush of warmth ran through her. How kind of him. A man kind enough to think of these little ones had to be a saint.

She handed out the candy to the accompaniment of giggles and *thank you's*. The dogs grabbed their bones from her hands and ran off to either chew on them or hide them from any bone thieves that happened along.

Aimee sat on the nearest porch step, surrounded by Maria and some of her friends. Gabe hadn't made an appearance. She hoped he was at school, and not working.

"How have you all been?"

"Good! We missed you."

"I told you before, I can't come every day. But I hold you in my special thoughts when I'm not here." Aimee paused, looking around to see if there were any adults nearby. She saw none. "Have you seen the policeman?"

The smiles disappeared. Nobody answered.

"Has he been here lately?"

A little boy of about five-years old spoke up. "We're not s'posed to talk about that."

Even the children are afraid. "Why not?"

"Because. Papa said so." He got up from the stoop and ran away.

Aimee sat in silence while the children enjoyed their candy. In a few moments, an older woman from two houses away opened her door and called something out in Spanish. The children all ran off, leaving her wondering what to do next.

CHAPTER FIVE

On Monday evening, Luke's mother finally called. His father's angioplasty had gone well and he was back in his hospital room, resting. Luke had looked up the procedure on the Internet and learned the use of angioplasty in the treatment of heart problems was quite common. The surgeons wound a catheter into his father's vein through an incision near the groin. Then they used a balloon to dilate any blockages in the arteries of his heart. This restored blood flow, thereby minimizing the damage to the heart muscle.

The articles Luke had read made it sound as routine as a tonsillectomy. Why, then, did he feel the need to be there with his mother at his dad's bedside? Where was his faith? He knew God was sovereign and the situation rested in His hands. His parents lived out that faith in their lives. Yet *his* faith sometimes wavered under the pressure of life's storms. *Is faith something only developing with age and experience?* He hoped not. He wanted that total trust in the Lord, *now*.

His phone rang and he perked up when he heard Aimee's voice on the other end of the line. "Aimee! I didn't expect to hear from you so soon."

***

Aimee's heart dropped. Had she called too soon? Was she making a nuisance of herself? She thought he'd want to hear about her visit with the children. Not that she had anything significant to report. "I can call back at another time, If you like."

"No. Don't hang up. I needed to hear your voice to cheer me up."

Luke needed cheering? And he thought she could do it? Apparently he wasn't aware of her mostly gloomy existence. "Why do you need cheering up?"

"My dad is in the hospital. A couple of thousand miles from here."

"Is it something serious?"

"Yes. No. I'm not sure. I guess he's stable right now. I tend to worry too much, I guess. Are you close to your parents?"

"My mother is no longer living."

"And your dad?"

The last thing Aimee wanted to do was talk about her father. It wasn't as if she were a part of his life anymore. "Uh . . . my father and I are not close.

"Oh. I'm sorry. I didn't mean to bring up a painful subject."

"It's not a painful subject," she denied. "Besides, we were talking about your father, remember?" *If he only knew the truth. Would he still be talking to me now?*

"I thought I detected something in your voice. I guess I didn't. Changing the subject, what did you call me about?"

"I visited the children at the orchard this afternoon."

"I know they must have enjoyed that."

Aimee warmed to Luke's words. He always believed the best about her. Nobody else treated her like he did. Certainly her father hadn't. "I brought them candy."

"I'll bet they enjoyed your company as much as they did the sweets." He paused, and then said in a low voice, "I know I would."

"You wouldn't say that if you knew me better."

"Why don't you give me a chance to know you better, and let me be the judge?"

Aimee chose to skip over that question. He wouldn't like her answer, anyway. "I tried to get them to talk about the deputy."

"And?"

"They wouldn't tell me anything. In fact, I got the impression they'd been told not to."

51

"Do you think their parents know you've been asking questions?"

"No. I only think they've been told not to talk about him to anyone." Aimee didn't know if Luke would have a solution, but if anyone would, it would be him.

"I'll be going there on Sunday morning. I've invited the entire community to come to church, and several of my friends are bringing vehicles to transport them. Why don't you come to?"

This was his answer? To go to church? "I'm really not much for churchgoing."

"How do you know if you've never gone?"

"Oh I've gone. All my life, in fact. Until . . ."

"Until what?"

The kindness in Luke's voice warmed her. Not condemnation. Not *holier than thou*. Simply kindness. She didn't know how to respond to that.

"It's a long story, Luke. One I'd rather not go in to."

"OK. I still think it would be great if you'd come with us on Sunday. The children will enjoy having you there with them. Your presence may even make it easier for them to feel at ease."

Why did he have to make saying no so difficult?

"Please, Aimee?"

"I'll try."

"Good. I'm looking forward to seeing you then."

"I hope you get good news about your father soon."

"Thank you, Aimee. Prayer does wonders, you know. The Lord will take care of everything."

Aimee said goodbye and hung up. There was no way Luke would be seeing *her* on Sunday.

The next Sunday morning, several men from church met at a prearranged spot with their vehicles, to caravan and pick up the families. Before heading out, the drivers gathered around to pray for the people they'd be meeting for the first

52

time. Luke's heart soared when he saw how many of his friends turned out for the outreach opportunity.

They climbed into their vehicles and with Luke leading, drove north, then wound their way up the hill to the orchards. Luke's excitement built with each curve and bend of the road. How many families would be waiting for them? They were bringing transportation for the majority, but in reality, Luke guessed only four or five families would come with them the first Sunday. Once word spread, more would join.

He hoped to gain their confidence and eventually gather enough information to stop the harassment from the deputy. Most of all, he wanted them to come to a personal relationship with Jesus Christ.

Luke recognized the last bend in the road. They were almost there. He could feel his smile splitting his face in half and figured he must look like a fool, but didn't care. At last, the row of houses came into view. Nobody waited outside. However, given the freezing temperatures, they were probably watching from their windows.

He pulled up and parked in front of Juan's house. The other vehicles pulled in behind him. What a sight their parade up the hill must have been. Luke hopped from his van and opened the sliding side door in readiness.

He hoped Aimee would be among the group. She hadn't said she wouldn't. But then she hadn't exactly jumped at the opportunity either. Juan's front door swung open, revealing Carmelita and her two children, Gabe and Maria.

"Carmelita, why don't you sit in back with your children, and Juan can sit up front with me. It will give us a chance to get to know one another better."

"My husband isn't coming."

Luke's smile froze, like a pose held too long for a slow photographer. A disappointment, but making a big deal out of Juan's absence might make the others feel unwelcome.

53

Juan would come next time after he heard what a blessing it had been for his family and neighbors.

"Please tell him how much I had looked forward to seeing him again."

Carmelita nodded and ushered her two children into the back of the van. The sound of opening car doors behind him told him that his friends looked forward to getting their passengers as well. Luke glanced down the row of houses, looking for more families.

Mitch came up behind him. "Where are the others? Should we knock on the doors?"

Luke pondered the suggestion. "The only family I'm actually acquainted with is this one. My contact, Aimee, tells me they are somewhat suspicious of strangers." He leaned over his driver's seat. "Carmelita, do you know who else is coming? From which houses?" He motioned to the houses with his hand. "The other drivers can round everybody up."

"I don't think anyone is going to come."

"Why not?" Discouragement overcame him when he realized what a difficult task he'd taken on. Even worse, his failure in front of his church family caused an embarrassed flush to rise from his face to the roots of his hair.

"They wouldn't fit in."

"Of course they would! We are all God's children and everybody is welcome in His church."

"Our families are not welcome in town."

"Carmelita, where did you get that idea. You are all welcome. And you'll be with us. Like special guests."

"I know you're our friend, but everybody is not like you."

Luke knew it would do no good to knock on doors that morning. All he could do is pray that those who did come would return and spread the word about how welcome they'd been made. He turned to Mitch. "Would you tell the others we won't have any more passengers this time?"

"Sure, buddy." He lightly cuffed Luke's shoulder to show his support. "Don't feel bad. I'm sure interest will pick up."

"I hope so." *Lord, show me the way. Even Aimee isn't here this morning. I want to serve you, but I feel discouraged right now.*

Carmelita insisted on sitting in the back of Luke's van with her children, leaving the passenger seat up front empty. Luke navigated back down the hill with his precious cargo, wishing like everything that Aimee were sitting beside him in that vacant seat. Why hadn't she come? He knew she cared as much for these families as he did. It had to be church she objected to. She'd given him enough reason to think so. If he had asked her to a different event, would she have come then?

Luke wondered why, if she had attended church her entire life, she stopped? And what kind of church would allow one of their members to drop out like that? Even a church as large as his, any member would be followed up on if they missed a few Sundays. How else could they meet the needs of God's family? Communication and caring counted. Maybe her church hadn't been like that.

Luke hoped her hiatus from the things of God, was only temporary. She'd come back soon if he had anything to say about it. First of all, she *needed* the Lord. Secondly, he wanted to see her happy and fulfilled which would only come with the first need. And, Luke admitted to himself, she had become an important part of his life . . . even though they'd never actually met in person.

Conversation in Spanish from behind him reached his ears. Since he didn't speak their language, he felt a little left out. They must feel like that every time they are away from their families. He'd make sure they were made welcome that day. Then he'd make another trip to meet all the other families.

55

He returned to his thoughts of Aimee. They'd talk face to face soon. He'd make meeting her a priority. Perhaps Carmelita could help arrange it.

Luke wished he had asked Matt's wife to ride with them. It hadn't even occurred to him. He'd counted on Aimee coming with them to help alleviate any discomfort or shyness among the families, especially the children. The further away they drove from the orchards, the more tension he sensed from the back of his van.

Hadn't they ever been gone into the city before? It didn't make sense. On one hand, they were brave and hardy people. They'd traveled thousands of miles from home to live in substandard conditions for very little compensation. According to Juan and Carmelita, they felt unwelcome. Luke didn't understand the prejudice against them. Nobody wanted the jobs they had. Nobody from the city would work long hours, doing backbreaking work, for such little pay. Yet these people returned year after year.

According to Mitch, they lived in their small communities, isolated from the very people who benefited from their labor. They didn't bother anyone. When their frustrations turned to violence, it was against each other.

Luke sensed hopelessness when he'd visited the orchards. He doubted if anyone had dreams of college for their children. In fact, it appeared that very few completed high school.

When they pulled into the church parking lot the conversation from the rear of the van stopped. Matt's wife and two of the other wives came over to the van to escort everybody inside. She took Maria and Gabe to the education wing where strains of lively music could already be heard. Carmelita stayed close to Luke and they entered the sanctuary where the congregation raised their voices in joyful praise choruses. Even though the lyrics were projected onto a large screen in front of the sanctuary, Carmelita did not

56

join in the singing. For all he knew, she couldn't read English.

The morning's sermon centered on each Christian's responsibility to share one another's burdens. The subject gave Luke renewed resolve to give his friendship to those less fortunate then himself. He noticed Carmelita paid close attention to everything and bowed her head for prayer when appropriate.

When the service was over, she seemed anxious to get back with her children, so Luke quickly ushered her out to the foyer. While they waited for Mitch's wife to bring the children to them, several women approached and introduced themselves. Though shy, Carmelita graciously acknowledged each introduction.

The children ran up, waving pictures and jumping up and down in excitement. "We had a good time, Mama. Can we come again? They told us stories and sometimes they have movies."

"We'll see. It's up to Papa."

Luke saw their mother looked pleased, but she was anxious to get home again. After saying goodbye to the people gathered around them, Luke took them to his van. Again, he asked Carmelita to sit in front with him, but she declined.

Maria and Gabe chattered all the way back to the orchards. Would the others be waiting to hear their report? Maybe even Aimee? He stopped in front of the cabins, and got out to open their door. As they stepped from his van, he noticed a county patrol vehicle driving slowly by.

CHAPTER SIX

Late Sunday night Aimee woke to the sound of sirens. They seemed unusually close. This wailing was different than the sirens she sometimes heard out on the main highway. These were close enough to rouse her from sleep.

She jumped out of bed and ran to the window. In the distance, she could see flashes of pulsating red lights through the cover of trees. *That's the orchard road!* She quickly dressed and ran outside to get her bike. When she saw the accumulation of snow, she realized the futility of trying to ride her bike. Especially uphill. She rushed back for her heavy boots.

The sound of sirens continued up the hill, and then stopped.

Oh, God, please don't let it be bad. Then she realized she'd actually prayed. How long had it been since she'd done that? Since the time of the accident. Well, conceivably God cared about all the children on the hill. At least she'd been taught that as a child. *Jesus loves the little children.* It had only been when she grew older that she realized how vengeful and unforgiving He could be.

By the time she reached the top of the hill, each breath she took came in deep sharp gulps. She could see the red lights in the distance, and the acrid smell of smoke reached her nostrils. When she finally reached the area where the families lived, the scene bustled with activity. She strained to see where the smoke was coming from. The firemen were gathered at the cabin on the end. The one right next to Juan and Carmelita's. Although the front door stood open, the firemen had congregated around the side of the little cabin.

From her vantage point, Aimee could see all the families huddled together. Their faces, in the eerie flashing lights, exhibited shock and fear. She crept closer. Was the

58

deputy there? She knew he patrolled the area at nighttime. Looking around, she failed to see any vehicles that did not belong, except for the two fire trucks. She circled around behind the trucks, trying to hear what was being said. However, the sound of the water pump on one of the trucks drowned out any conversation she might have heard.

At least no flames were visible. The fire appeared to be out, and only the stench of burning wood remained. What could have happened? What, or who, would start a fire outside someone's home in the middle of the night?

Aimee knew she'd be no help to those people so turned and made her way back home. She had to call Luke.

***

When the phone rang so late at night, Luke's gut told him it would be more bad news. Might be a good subject for his column. *Why doesn't good news ever come between midnight and five o'clock in the morning?*

The sound of Aimee's voice immediately put his mind at ease regarding his Dad's health. However, her reason for calling at that hour had to be just as urgent.

"Aimee, what is it?"

"There's been a fire . . . at the orchards. Somebody tried to burn down one of the cabins."

"Arson? Are you sure? Could it have been faulty wiring? Or a spark from a wood stove?" Luke's impression of the cabins told him that money hadn't been spent to secure safe housing for the farm workers.

"The fire started *outside* the cabin. Who would do such a thing? People's lives could have been lost. Do you have any idea how many children live there?"

"I suppose it could be our friend, the deputy. If he'd been around, he would have seen all our cars there this morning. I'm sure I saw him drive past when I dropped Carmelita and her kids off."

"That would mean he's a potential murderer!"

"Was anyone hurt?"

"No. But what if nobody had noticed the fire? What then? Somebody could have died."

"If it was the deputy, he probably meant it as a warning." Luke's guilt for bringing any retaliation on the small Hispanic community rose from his stomach and threatened to cut off his air. "This could be my fault."

"I'm sure it's not. As you know, bad things happen up there all the time. It could have been someone from one of the other camps who has a grudge. This isn't your fault."

Luke had been so focused on this particular group of people, he hadn't even considered all the other places in the area where people lived in the same squalid conditions. It was only when Aimee had brought it up that he realized the orchard situation wasn't unique. He wanted to help them all, but seemed to have made a mess of trying to help the ones he knew.

"Luke? What should we do? I'm worried about their safety."

"I'm going to call the prayer chain. The Lord protected them from harm tonight. We'll pray He continues to do so."

"I was hoping you'd have some concrete ideas. If I have to, I'll stand guard over them myself." Aimee spit her words out, clearly letting Luke know what she thought of the prayer chain.

"Aimee, I didn't say I wasn't going to do anything else. Call me at the office tomorrow. I need some time to think and pray about this."

Luke didn't hear Aimee say goodbye before she hung up. At least she hadn't slammed her receiver down. But was her anger directed toward him or toward God? Or both?

Aimee's bitterness ran deep, but Luke wasn't ready to give up on her. He'd come to care for her a great deal. He'd manage to break down her walls eventually.

***

Monday morning, Aimee woke to icy sleet pounding against her bedroom window. She pulled the covers up around her shoulders and face. The timer on her furnace wasn't set to turn it on for another hour. Staying in bed, snug and warm, held a lot of appeal. At least her cupboards were full, so she didn't have to go outside and drive on slick streets.

A gust of wind hit the side of the house, rattling the windows. How could anyone go back to sleep with all the noise? Even though she'd stayed up late the night before, working on her verses and cards, going back to sleep was out of the question. She reluctantly crawled out of bed and put on her flannel robe.

Her fingers turned to icicles before she got her heavy socks and slippers on. She hurried out of her cold bedroom to turn on the heat. Before long, the little house warmed up and the teakettle whistled, indicating she probably wouldn't freeze to death after all. *If heating fuel weren't so expensive, I would leave the heat on all night.*

She poured hot water over the bag of spiced tea she'd purchased on her last trip to the store. Glancing out the window, she noticed the sleet was mixed with snow and it had already spread a blanket of white over the trees and bushes. She'd harvested her last vegetables in time.

Loud ringing from the other room interrupted the silence. Aimee rushed to answer the phone on the off chance it was Mrs. Crow calling and not someone seeking donations.

"Hello?"

"Aimee, are you sitting down?"

It was Mrs. Crow! "You got the sketches. Did you like them?" Aimee didn't sit down. Instead, she shifted her weight from one foot to the other and back again, in hopeful anticipation. She'd spent an entire day on her new idea, taking a chance on something fresh, instead of working on her tried and true designs.

"Yes, I received them. Why else would I be calling?"

To tell me I'd missed my deadline? That I wouldn't be getting a check this month? She wouldn't exactly starve, since she'd been so frugal, but it would cut into her precious savings. It would cause her to put off her goal of her plastic surgery, and ultimately beginning a real relationship with someone like Luke. Maybe even Luke himself.

The editor didn't wait for Aimee's answer. "We want to give you a new contract."

Uh, oh. They're cutting back.

"I showed your new work to our editorial board and to marketing. They want to develop an entire new line of products featuring your sketches. Cards, calendars, mugs, T-shirts, maybe even framed prints . . . the works."

Aimee sat down. She had hoped for good news. She never dreamed it would be *that* good.

"Aimee?"

"Does this mean more money?"

"Well, it depends on sales, of course. But I have no doubt the public will love your children like we do. You'll get a flat fee for your cards like before, but the pay you'll get for the gift items with the same drawings on them, will be above and beyond the flat fee. It's a royalty contract."

Aimee cradled the phone in her left hand, and with her right hand, she passed her fingertips over her scarred face. The time for her transformation was getting closer. The time for penance was nearly over.

"We need more of the same kind from you as soon as possible. They're anxious to get into production."

Aimee hesitated. How could she increase her output and keep an eye on things up the hill at the same time? "How many different drawings do you need?"

"At least a couple of dozen. Then we can pick out the most marketable ones."

"I'll do my best."

"I'll call you back in a few days to see how you're progressing. And one more thing . . . we love your verses. They nearly sound as if taken straight out of the Bible."

Aimee felt heat rise in her face. How ironic. She no longer had God's favor, but her years attending Sunday school had imprinted His word in her mind. She agreed to start right away, still wondering how she'd manage the extra work. However, the opportunity was too big to pass up. She'd been saving for her surgery for years. She could almost taste the joy she'd get from looking in the mirror and not being reminded of the night she was driving the car. The night her mother died because Aimee skidded off the road.

She no longer cared if her father would think she was vain about her looks. That she deserved the reminder. Now she had another reason for wanting the scars removed. Luke. Aimee pulled her savings passbook out of her desk drawer. She'd saved nearly half of what she needed. Most of it had been deposited the last two years when she began selling her greeting cards. Now, it could be a matter of months and she'd have enough to make an appointment with the plastic surgeon.

Slipping the folder back in her desk, she debated asking Luke to check in on the people at the orchards. Maybe if he'd stop by there in the evening, after dark, she could set her alarm and check again around midnight.

Aimee reached for the phone, then pulled back her hand. Nothing had changed since she last spoke with him. He probably *did* pray about the situation. That was fine. But how far would he be willing to go, to not only protect defenseless people, but to catch the deputy in the act of doing something illegal?

63

Aimee decided to do as much as she could by herself and only call Luke if he were absolutely needed. If he tried to draw her into another conversation about God, he'd surely be disappointed in her lack of enthusiasm. She didn't want to tell him his faith had never been tested. If it had been, he wouldn't be so naive about praying about everything . . . as if God were some great vending machine in the sky.

Winter along with heavy snowfalls would be present soon. Aimee wouldn't be able to trudge up and down the steep hill several times each night. *Besides, how fast could I get to a phone if something bad happened? I'm sure none of the families have a phone.*

A thought occurred to her. It would be no big sacrifice to spend some of her savings for a cell phone. The families on the hill were the closest thing to a family she had. If she got a prepaid phone, she wouldn't be locked into a contract. She got dressed to take the drive to a nearby mall. There was an office supply and electronics store there, where she'd seen just the phone she'd need.

Aimee mulled over the decision to drive that early in the morning, or wait until the roads had cleared. Experience told her she'd run into fewer people if she didn't wait until after lunch. She got ready to go.

A little while later she turned south onto the highway that ran parallel to the Columbia River. There was ice in the shady patches, but for the most part the road was clear. Still, her hands gripped the steering wheel as if her fingers alone would keep her out of a skid. Would she ever be able to relax again while driving? Years had passed since her accident. She heaved a sigh of relief when she reached the outskirts of the city where the speed limit reflected her comfort zone.

A traffic signal ahead of her turned red and she eased her car to a stop. Cars crossed the intersection in front of her, presumably carrying people on their way to work. How

64

lucky she felt that she could work at home, and not make that drive every day. The last vehicle through turned South . . . the same direction she was traveling. Her heart lurched into her throat when she realized it was Luke.

The light turned green, and she found herself right behind him. If he looked into his rear-view mirror, he'd see her. However, he didn't know what she, or her car, looked like, so she wouldn't attract his attention. The blood in her veins pumped through a little faster. Being this close warmed her, even though it was difficult to see him through the tinted windows of the van.

Aimee imagined what it would be like riding along with him. Sharing a conversation while making occasional eye contact, without worrying what her face looked like. They might even stop somewhere for coffee. She could tell him about her call from Mrs. Crow.

Her destination loomed ahead, only a block away. She hated to turn off. But what was she going to do? Follow him all the way to his office? Flag him down and introduce herself? Watch him cringe away in horror when he saw her monster face?

Nope, she wanted to be beautiful, or at the least half pretty, the first time he saw her. And it could be within the year. All she had to do between now and then was avoid being in the same place at the same time as Luke.

CHAPTER SEVEN

Luke exhaled as he pulled away from the newspaper parking lot. He'd spent all of Monday grinding out enough columns for several days. He'd turned them in to the editor Tuesday morning and they'd been accepted. Now, on Tuesday afternoon, he could give his full attention to the goings on at Cherry Orchard Road.

The sun shown brightly, reflecting off crisp white snow. It had snowed steadily since Monday morning, leaving a foot of new accumulation. Then the storm had passed as quickly as it had arrived.

Luke vowed to keep ahead of his office workload so he'd have the freedom to respond to any trouble at the Orchards. The fire on Sunday night had scared him and Aimee both. He couldn't imagine how upsetting it had been for the people on the hill. From now on, he'd check on them several times a week. He'd also keep an eye out for that deputy. Now that he knew his presence there was perfectly legal, he wouldn't allow himself to be intimidated by a gun and a uniform.

Aimee hadn't called him back since the night of the fire. The entire issue of her keeping her phone number from him, gnawed at him till his heart felt raw. What possible reason could she have for being so illusive? She had nothing to fear from him. He only wanted to stay in close touch.

Cherry Orchard road hadn't been plowed, but tracks from other vehicles, probably including the bus, had tamped it down so his studded tires easily kept him from slipping. He looked forward to getting there, accessing the fire damage, and offering whatever assistance he could provide. Luke had already called Mitch and some others from church, and they had agreed to come with tools and lumber if necessary.

He rounded the last bend and spotted a dozen or so children gathered in front of Juan and Carmelita's cabin. An adult he didn't recognize stood in their midst, and by the way they were hanging on her, she was someone they adored. She turned and glanced toward his vehicle, spun around, and vaulted up the steps to the cabin. Before he could stop his van, she disappeared inside.

***

Aimee's feet refuse to move. They were glued in place when she realized trying to escape would be impossible. There was no way out without Luke seeing her. The friendship they'd built over the little time they'd known each other, would never survive if she ran away again.

On the other hand, any possible future with him would be out of the question once he saw her gruesome face. Perhaps it was only fitting she lose Luke. After all, her mother had lost everything because of her . . . her future, her family, and the most fundamental loss of all, her life.

Maybe there's a way. Aimee gathered up her coat, scarf, and gloves. She peeked through the window. His swift walk from his vehicle brought him closer, and he would be there any moment. Even from inside, she could hear the children calling out to her, *Angel! Angel!*

She hurried to slip the heavy jacket on, zipping it all the way up, and turning the collar up around her neck. She jammed her hands in each pocket until she found her wool ski cap. Just as Luke reached the porch, she pulled it over her head. The cap had been designed with the coldest weather in mind. Only her eyes and mouth showed. The rest of her face was hidden. The scars didn't show. Could she get away with it?

She took a deep breath and stepped outside where hopefully, her coverings wouldn't be questioned. She could bluff her way through this.

"Luke! I didn't know you were coming. The children and I were just on our way to go sledding. Let's go, children!" They scampered away. "Juan is inside, if you're here to see him."

"Juan can wait. Don't you think it's about time we met face to face? You seem to have the advantage since you apparently know what I look like." He took one long stride and stood inches from her on the porch. Closer than he'd ever been. He reached toward her.

Aimee's heart lurched. She thought it would jump out of her chest. She let him take her hand, but feared he'd detect her trembling, so pulled it away again.

"The children are waiting for me. It will be dark soon."

"If you won't stay and talk to me, then I'll just have to come with you."

"But you're not dressed for the cold." She pointedly eyed his light jacket. Unlike her ski gloves, his were black leather driving gloves. Even his shoes were more appropriate for an office than a snowy hill.

"You're not getting rid of me that easily. I carry warm outer wear in my van just for occasions like this." He reached out and fingered a lock of her hair that had escaped from her cap.

It was all she could do to keep from cringing backward. "Won't Juan wonder why you've gone off and deserted him?"

"I think he'll understand when I explain."

"OK. I'll see you on the hill then." Aimee escaped before Luke could object. The temptation to flee down the hill to her house warred with her desire to spend time with Luke. *With all the children around, it should be easy to keep a safe distance between us, and still give the illusion of being friendly.*

She trotted around the house and climbed the hill to where the children waited. Some of the older ones had already taken their first plunge down the steeper slope, and were pulling their makeshift sleds of pieces of wood and rope behind them as they ascended again. The younger ones amused themselves by spinning around the lower area atop plywood-topped inner tubes. Aimee had brought nothing to slide on, but instead had brought her sketch pad and pencils. She hoped to catch the joyous mood of the children as they slid, fell, and laughed in the new fallen snow.

The noise of the dogs barking in excitement added to the noise of the shouting, giggling, children, so Aimee didn't hear Luke approach.

"What are you working on?" His voice rumbled behind her.

She covered her work with her hand, not wanting to put her chicken scratches on display. "Oh. I'm merely amusing myself while I watch the children."

"Are you babysitting, or guarding them?"

Aimee knew full well what he meant. "A little of both, I guess. Although I find it hard to believe anyone would hurt these precious little ones."

He sat down beside her on the log. "So you've changed your mind since the other night? You think the fire was an accident?"

"It was no accident. I looked at the place the fire started. There was a pile of newspapers there, half burned."

"Perhaps they'd taken them out in the garbage."

"These were newspapers from town. Nobody up here reads those. I asked around."

Aimee returned to her sketching, but noted Luke's long pause. The way her hands still trembled at his nearness, there was no way she would be sending these drawings to Mrs. Crow.

"Aimee." He dipped his head toward her. "Your hair has almost red highlights mixed with the brown. And it's so long. It must be beautiful under that cap. Could you take it off? I'd like to see the face of the person I've gotten to know so well over the phone."

She could feel the goose bumps travel up her arms. His voice. His tenderness. She guessed no woman had ever refused him anything. Still . . .

"Please?"

"Luke, I don't dare. Between the sun bouncing off the snow, and the cold air, I have to keep my face protected or I'll regret it tomorrow."

"Not even for a moment?"

How had she gotten herself in such a predicament? She turned toward him, pleading with him with her gaze.

Luke pulled in a huge breath. "Your eyes are beautiful! As is your mouth, what I can see of it. I know under all that heavy wool, the rest of you is beautiful too. I know for sure your heart is."

Aimee felt as giddy as a school girl when he kept piling on the compliments. "You're very kind."

Luke put his arm around her shoulders, making her freeze in place for fear the feeling of warmth would end. No man had ever shown her affection. Sure, she'd had boyfriends in high-school. She'd gone on a few dates in her senior year. Of course they were with boys her parents approved of. Boys from their church. But they were boys. This was a man.

Aimee knew she could get used to the feeling of being protected. Luke was the kind of man who would make anyone feel safe and cared for. That was why she had to be so careful not to scare him away. She jumped up.

"Let's get a little closer to the children. I'd like to draw them from a different vantage point." She grabbed her sketch pad which had fallen to the ground.

Months of bicycling and walking up and down Cherry Orchard Road had strengthened her legs to the point most people would have a difficult time keeping up with her.

70

Luke, with his long stride seemed to be an exception. He kept up with her, clear to the top of the hill which the children used as the staging area for their downhill slides.

She stopped, kneeling down to draw Gabe who sat poised on his improvised sled, made of cardboard. Luke passed her up, walking directly to Gabe. He pulled out his wallet and gave the boy a dollar bill. Gabe stood, his grin as wide as the Columbia as he took the money.

"What are you doing, Luke?" She hoped his idea of making friends with families didn't include handing out cash. These people had too much pride for that.

"I'm renting us a sled."

What is he talking about? That's not a sled and this isn't a ski resort.

Luke took three giant strides and tugged her to her feet. "Come on."

Aimee half stumbled along as he pulled her toward Gabe's piece of cardboard. Surely he didn't mean for her to slide down that hill. Before she could get her footing again, Luke sat her on the cardboard and arranged himself behind her, a leg on each side of her.

"OK, Gabe. Push us off!"

Aimee looked down at the long expanse of icy hill in front of her and nearly panicked. She wanted to clutch onto something, but the only thing available were Luke's knees. More boys ran up to help Gabe push and they slowly got underway. Next thing she knew, they were streaking down the hill at speeds she was sure approached the speed of sound. It must have been, because she couldn't even hear herself scream.

Luke's arms surrounded her and his laughter rang in her ears. Before they hit bottom, she started to laugh along with him. She'd never felt so carefree.

Several children surrounded them as they lay sprawled on the snow. "Take me next time! Take me!" Their voices echoed across the valley.

"Yes, Luke. Take them. I couldn't stand another trip down that hill." Aimee laughed, watching the children tumble over Luke like puppies.

"I'm afraid you'll run away if I leave you."

"I promise to stay at least an hour. I really want to do some sketches."

"He helped Aimee to her feet. "I'll hold you to that promise." His eyes twinkled, and when the corner of his mouth turned up, deep dimples formed delightful grooves in his face. She hadn't been able to see those from a distance.

The children tugged on his hands, pulling him up the hill. He looked over his shoulder and winked at her. "I'll be back."

Pleasure coursed through her, warming her from the inside out. She watched them make their way up the hill. Grabbing her sketch pad again, she settled herself back on the log and drew dozens of different scenes. *Some of these could be used for Christmas cards.* The screaming laughter coming from the slope reminded her of the joyful times she'd had in the snow as a child. Her father had taken her sledding, taking her down the hill the same way as Luke had done here.

Aimee seldom allowed herself to think of those days. She still missed her mom, but the deep grieving had passed. Replaced by guilt and the pain of her father's rejection. It had been several years since she'd left his house and moved away. Did he ever have any regrets? Perhaps that she'd ever been born?

Aimee wondered if she'd ever be reconciled to her father. But he had ignored her pleas. She'd finally given up trying. Since then, she'd been trying hard to be worthy, both as a person and worthy to God. Surely He couldn't keep his back turned to her forever.

"Ha! Caught you daydreaming." Luke stood in front of her and she hadn't even heard him approach.

"Guilty as charged." Aimee couldn't help responding to his teasing. She glanced behind him. No little crumb grabbers were latched on to him this time. He had his full attention on her.

"Have you warmed up enough to take that cap off yet?"

Aimee hugged herself as if to say the cold still affected her. She watched him warily, hoping he wouldn't press the issue . . . worse yet, pull her cap off in his teasing.

He plopped down next to her again. "Would you mind showing me what you're working on?"

Aimee flipped her notebook back to the beginning pages which were full of playing, laughing children. She didn't show him the sketch she'd done of him, surrounded by the crowd of little ones as if he were the Pied Piper. She'd torn that one out and put it in her knapsack.

Luke silently turned each page, spending time studying each one. "These are really very good. Have you ever thought of selling your artwork?"

"I do a little freelancing." She didn't want to give him too many details. "So how is your job going? Do you like it?"

"Yes and no." He looked intently into her eyes. "It's not very challenging, and quite honestly, not very meaningful."

"I love your columns. I always look forward to reading them. I never guess what subjects you will be covering next."

"Thanks. But I'd like to do more serious writing. I'd like to think I could make a difference in the world."

"Like how?"

"Like writing about these children. Their lives. Their families. The hardships they face merely trying to put food on the table."

"Why don't you do it?"

"Our managing editor seems to want to avoid any controversial subjects. He wants straight reporting and fluff."

"I'll bet if you wrote something up and he saw how good it was, he'd change his mind."

Luke laughed, but it wasn't a happy laugh. "He's made it abundantly clear I am to stick with what he hired me to do."

"There are other newspapers."

"And I may be forced to move to one. It's hard to break in, though. There's not a big demand for my type of column. Not when they can get syndicated columns by well known writers."

Luke handed the sketch pad back to Aimee. She set it on her lap, her hands resting on the cover.

"Aimee, I can't begin to tell you how great it is to spend this time with you. I'd like to do it more often. When can I see you again?"

"My schedule is full right now. But it won't always be that way."

"Are you saying you'd like to spend time with me, too?" Luke reached for her hand.

Aimee's hand tingled, like tiny jolts of electricity pulsing through her fingers. Luke's touch gave her hope for the day hiding from him would be unnecessary. She'd never had those feelings before. She wanted him to remove his hand from hers, and to keep it there, never letting her go, all at the same time.

"I'd like that," she answered, keenly aware of his thumb caressing her palm.

"When could I take you out for dinner? I know a place with excellent food and service, where I'd love to take you."

"Someday. But not now."

"Don't you ever eat dinner? You must be skin and bones under that heavy coat." Luke's grin told her he was teasing her a little.

Aimee laughed. "Of course I don't. How did you think I stayed so slim?"

"How would I know if you're slim or fat under all the coats and scarves and caps?"

"I guess I'll just have to keep you guessing for a while longer."

Luke squeezed her hand. She wanted to grip his in return. She would gladly keep him with her always, to keep the nightmares, and every other hurtful thing away. Instead she withdrew her hand and stood.

"It's getting dark. Time for the children to be getting back home." She clutched her notebook to her chest.

Luke stood too. "Can I take you home?"

"I need to visit a little with some of the families. I'm not sure how soon I'll be ready to go home."

"OK. I'll be talking with Juan. Why don't you come get me when you're ready?"

Aimee, Luke and the children returned to the cabins. She watched Luke enter Juan's cabin. She'd be long gone when he came out.

CHAPTER EIGHT

Aimee called Luke the next day to see if he had learned anything from Juan. As usual, his voice sent butterflies fluttering around in her stomach.

"He seems to think the fire was an accident."

"Do you believe him?"

"Let's just say I'm reserving my opinion."

No matter what Juan said, and what Luke believed, she knew the fire was no accident. Rehashing it wouldn't change anything.

"I had a wonderful time yesterday." She might as well change the subject.

"Yeah, but I wish you wouldn't have run out on me."

"I got a sudden chill and had to get home and into a hot shower."

"I was so intent on my visit with Juan, I didn't even hear you drive away."

Aimee didn't contradict him. As long as he thought she'd driven, he wouldn't figure out how close she lived.

"What kind of car do you have? I'll watch for you."

"Nothing to brag about. Just an old clunker. Tell me about your visit with Juan."

"I thought it went very well, considering everything that has gone on. I couldn't get him to open up about the deputy, though."

"Nobody there wants to move away. They desperately need their jobs. They don't want to start all over in a new place."

"Is there any other possible reason he wouldn't talk to me?"

"Fear, obviously. Remember how he'd been beaten the first night you saw him? And then the fire. Who knows what else has happened we're not even aware of."

Things would be different for them now. A man like Luke would never let anything more happen to them if he could help it. *Imagine having a man like him permanently part of my life. I'd be safe and loved. His love for the migrants is so evident. And he doesn't even know them personally.*

"So when can we go sledding again?"

Aimee laughed, and Luke's chuckle joined in. He really did seem to have a much fun as she had.

"I think you may have enjoyed yourself even more than the children. Did you get to do much sledding as a child?"

"Nothing like what we did. It's not very mountainous where I grew up."

"I've been meaning to ask you . . . how is your father?"

"He's doing much better. You know, it means a lot that you asked."

"I could tell his hospitalization was difficult for you."

"Well, just being able to talk to you helped a lot."

She didn't know what to say. How could someone as insignificant as her make a difference in anyone's life?

"I was serious about seeing you again."

Aimee would like nothing better. Luke's arm around her was a memory she'd carry with her to her old age. Excitement built within her knowing it might only be months till she could say yes to Luke's invitations. She could even have him over for dinner. They'd go places together. Maybe even make plans for the future.

"Are you still there?"

"What? Oh, yes. I got distracted for a moment."

"I'm asking you for a date. Please don't tell me you'd turn me down and break my heart."

"You're teasing me again."

"I would never tease about something like that."

"Could you be patient for a while longer? And believe I'd like to go out with you if I could?"

"Aimee, I have to ask you something."

Oh no, he was going to put her in a corner. She stiffened, waiting for the question she probably couldn't answer.

"Go ahead."

"Is there another reason you won't go out with me? Are . . . are you married?"

"No! Why would you think such a thing?"

"It's just that I can't think of any good reason for us not to spend time together."

"We're spending time together right now."

"It's not the same. I want to see your face. Touch your hair. I'd like to see the expression in your eyes when we talk."

"Please believe me when I say I'd love to be able to carve out enough time for dates and outings on a sled, and whatever else you've suggested. It's not possible right now."

"But it will be in the future."

Aimee flinched. She hadn't convinced him. But there was nothing she could do about it."

"That's the way it has to be . . . for now."

"I guess I've got no choice but to accept that. Be advised, however, that I just may get tired of waiting and show up on your doorstep with a huge bouquet of flowers and an invitation you won't be able to decline."

"That gives me something to look forward to."

"I've got another call coming in. Will you call me back soon?"

"I promise."

Aimee didn't call him back for several days. She did keep an eye on the families up the hill. Every night as soon as it got dark, she traipsed up the hill to see if that deputy was lurking around. She always carried a couple of jars of preserves with her in case she was caught and needed an excuse for being there herself. She usually crept into the old school bus where she could observe yet be out of the wind. It would also be easy to hide there if someone drove up.

Luke wrote his Thanksgiving Day column and turned it in. Most everyone at the paper left early the day before the holiday and he did too. He had an important errand to run. Several families from church, who had offered their support in helping the people in the orchard, had gotten together and filled several baskets with food. The privilege of delivering them fell to him, since everyone else had company to prepare for.

Luke took the familiar drive up the hill and distributed the baskets to everyone who was home. Their pride went by the wayside when they saw the abundance of goodies and the love which went into assembling everything. His only regret was his inability to speak to Aimee and invite her along.

And she should have been with him. She was as much a part of showing love to those folks as anyone. They were beginning to work as a team. God had answered his prayer for a life partner. Sure there were a few things needing to be worked out, but he had not doubt that Aimee had been sent directly to him for a special reason.

If anyone had asked him, he wouldn't have been able to describe how he felt when he'd finally laid eyes on her. Like a lightening bolt had shot down from the sky and struck him numb. It was all he could do to keep from gathering her in his arms so all of his senses could experience her presence. All that and cupid's arrows too. He chuckled, remembering her joy during the sled run. To be so close, and not even see her face. And yet, he sensed her beauty. God's gift to him.

***

Aimee had thought the worst night of her life occurred when she'd skidded on the ice and wrecked her car, killing her mother in the process. Now she wondered how many of those *worst* nights she'd have to endure.

79

The ambulance, its lights flashing, pulled away from the cabins. As long as Aimee would live, she'd never forget the screams of the children. She'd had to lift Carmelita up from the ground when the fireman carried Maria from the smoke filled cabin. She'd nearly fainted herself when she realized the little girl hadn't escaped with the others. Gabe said she'd stopped to find her teddy bear. Aimee hoped Luke wouldn't find out why Maria didn't get out. He'd only blame himself for yet another tragedy he couldn't prevent.

Juan had gone in the ambulance with Maria. There hadn't been room for anyone else. *God, please let Maria live!* Her little face had been covered with an oxygen mask when they'd loaded her in. Her skin was as black as the blackened boards which were all that remained of their former home.

A sob caught in Aimee's throat. The deputy was no longer around. He'd disappeared before the emergency vehicles got there. But she'd seen him. She saw him with the gasoline can, running from the cabins. She didn't know if he'd seen her. She kept herself so well hidden, she almost had missed seeing him leave. He must have been there already when she arrived to take up her post inside the bus. Keeping watch had paid off. If she'd only arrived sooner. Little Maria would still be safe instead of on her way to the hospital.

As soon as it was safe, she'd report what she'd seen. Then she'd have to lay low till the arsonist had been put in jail.

Aimee offered to let Carmelita, Juan, and Gabe stay with her since their home was destroyed. Carmelita didn't know if Juan would agree. Besides he wouldn't know where to find her. Aimee gave her the cell phone she'd purchased. At least they'd be able to stay in contact that way.

A deputy Aimee had never seen before approached and offered to take the anxious mother and son to the hospital. Aimee waited till they left, then walked down the hill toward her home. Halfway down, she tripped and fell, blinded by tears. She rose again, wiping her eyes with the edge of her sleeve.

***

"Luke!"

Aimee's cry pierced his heart as he juggled the phone to his ear. She was crying hysterically. He could hardly understand a word she said.

"Calm down. What's happened?"

"Another fire. Maria is hurt." She stopped and sobbed some more.

"What happened? Were you there?"

"Yes. I saw him this time. It *was* that deputy. He did it. Oh that poor little girl! She looked so bad when they took her away."

"Did you tell anyone what you saw?"

"No yet. But I'll write it down and send it to the fire department. I heard someone say they were sending an arson investigator up there."

"Aimee, you have to report it right now. We can't let him get away with this!"

"I know. But I got scared he might be standing in the shadows and would see me. He's evil!"

"Where are you now?"

"At home."

"Did anyone see you there? At the orchard, I mean?"

"Juan did. I don't know if anyone else did or not. Except I did talk to one of the firemen, but only briefly. I don't remember if I even gave him my name. Everything was so chaotic."

"OK. Wait till you calm down a little, and then drive down to the sheriff's office. I'll meet you there."

"No! He might be there!"

"He can't do anything to you with everybody else around."

81

"He'll find me. Once he knows I was there, he'll come after me next."

"Then I'll meet you at the fire station. If I'm not mistaken, they have investigators who can arrest this guy. Then he won't have to see your face."

"I have to do it my way. If something happens to me, who will take care of all those people?"

"I won't let anything happen to you. I promise. I'll even find you a family to stay with until this is over."

"I'll think about it."

"Let me know. OK?" Luke heard her sob again and it felt like a knife twisting inside of him. He almost lost it when she hung up without saying goodbye.

***

Aimee cowered in the darkness of her living room. Several times a county patrol car had driven up and down the road at the end of her driveway. Was it him? She was positive he hadn't seen her that night. But a news reporter had overheard her talking to one of the firefighters. Then he'd written an article stating a witness had come forward. Had the deputy read it and somehow ferreted out her name and address? But how could he? Nobody knew her name and address.

Even thought she was blue with cold, she cracked the door so she could hear anyone approach. How she wished for Luke's presence. Yet there was no sense in putting him in danger too. The deputy already knew who he was. It was better if Luke stayed away. She could close her eyes and almost feel Luke's strong arms around her when they'd whooshed down the hill on the little cardboard sled. Her daydreams would have to suffice for now.

Aimee shivered. She'd give anything to find out the fire had only been one of her nightmares. Why did such awful things have to happen to her and the people she loved? Was God paying attention at all?

She had to get far away. Nobody was going to believe her story about the night of the fire. Why would they take her word against an officer of the law? A man sworn to protect.

She listened at the door again. Everything was quiet. She'd turned off her heat so there wouldn't be any smoke coming from the chimney. Additionally, with the lights out, she hoped anyone coming by would think none was home.

She crept into her bedroom, and pulled the old window shade to the sill. All she'd use for a light would be a candle. She didn't have a lot to pack anyway. A few items of clothing. She could practically gather those by feel. Her computer would have to go with her. It was her lifeline to her only source of income. She didn't know when she would be coming back, if ever.

No point in leaving a note. Who would come looking for her? Only the deputy.

She'd already decided where she was going. Maria was still in a burn unit in Seattle. She wanted to be nearby. She would find a room for rent and check the local news on the Internet each day to see if her name had been publicized. If she had to, she'd sell her car and change her name so she couldn't be found.

Aimee finished packing her suitcase and moved it out of the bedroom, closing the door behind her. She set about unhooking her computer. He fingers were so frozen, dealing with the connections were difficult. She cupped her hands around the candle, getting scant warmth from the glow, but it helped some.

She stuffed all the cords and cables into a paper bag and took it, and her suitcase, to her car. It was difficult making no noise, but *he* could be waiting and watching for her out there.

She made several more trips to carry her computer, monitor, printer and all her supplies.

Coming inside, Aimee took one more look around. Something scraped against a window. She jumped. *Was it him?* Her hands shook like aspen leaves. Standing perfectly still, she listened. She heard it again. Barely turning her head, she looked to the left, where the noise had come from. In the dim outside light, reflected from the snow, she saw the outline of a tree branch swaying in the wind. It hit the window, making the same noise she'd heard before.

Aimee gulped huge amounts of air, sobs welling up in her throat. She could taste her own fear and it made her want to gag. She rushed outside to the garage and pushed up the big door. Then she hurried to the drivers door, yanked it open and got in, locking her door and making sure all the other doors were locked too.

The old engine sputtered to life and she backed out. Knowing it was too late to hide, she switched on her headlights and sped down the driveway, not even stopping at the road, but turning toward the main highway.

Aimee drove toward Wenatchee, carefully obeying the speed limit. The sanding truck had gone before her, providing her with some measure of relief. But she knew she wouldn't feel altogether safe until she got over Steven's pass.

CHAPTER NINE

Any hope Luke had of finding Aimee decreased with each passing day. He didn't even know if she were dead or alive. The deputy, who set fire to Juan's house, could have just as well harmed Aimee. Had he learned she'd stumbled onto the truth and gone after her? The worse scenario, and the thought pierced his heart like a sword, was that she might be dead. It would be his fault. He should have discouraged her from going up there on her own instead of joining in the investigation. Once she had told him about the problems in the orchard, he should have told her to stay out of it. But no. He had to use any excuse to get close to her. His obsession had put her in jeopardy.

He'd tried contacting hospitals, but they treated him like some kind of crazy. And no wonder. He couldn't provide a decent description or a last name.

How had he fallen in love with someone he knew so little about? He couldn't explain it, but on a deep level, he knew God ordained the connection with her. But if that were really true, why had God brought her into his life and then snatch her away? Had he somehow failed God as well as Aimee?

He pulled into the parking lot of the Christian bookstore. The owner had ordered several books of Bible stories written in Spanish. He hoped they'd come in so he could take them to the orchards. Learning about God and His love for them might give them a lift after the tragedies they'd experienced. He also wanted to pick out a card for his Dad.

While he waited for the clerk to look for his order, he browsed through the get-well cards. Should he pick something lighthearted and funny? Or would his Dad prefer something with a message of hope and love? Luke picked through dozens of cards, looking for just the right one.

The clerk returned with the news that his books weren't in yet, but would be there by the end of the week.

He turned his attention back to the rack of cards. Maybe he should get several. Little Maria would be in the hospital for a long time. He should send her something weekly, to let her know he and the entire church were all praying for her.

Displayed on a separate turnstile rack, were various brightly colored cards. Luke stepped up to the rack, looking for something suitable for a young girl. He turned the rack and stopped as if paralyzed. The designs on those cards were identical to Aimee's. Had she copied them? Luke lifted a card out of its slot and turned it over to read the back. The company logo and copyright. Beneath it was stamped, *Designs by Aimee!* His heart sped up. One by one, he grabbed the cards off the rack till he had them all. He rushed to the counter and dropped them in front of the clerk.

"Do you know her? Aimee? She lives locally."

The clerk glanced at the cards. "We've carried that line for a couple of years. I didn't know the artist lived around here, though. How interesting."

"Is there a way to find out her last name? Her address?"

"I suppose you could contact the company, but I don't know if they'd give you that information."

Luke shifted his weight from foot to foot, several times. "Could you give me their phone number?"

"I don't have that information. We get our products from a central distributor."

Excited about his discovery, he paid for all the cards and left. He had a place to start looking for Aimee. *Lord I know you love her. Please keep her safe until I find her.*

He turned back the way he'd come and headed for his office. He had a computer on his desk, hooked up to the Internet. He'd never seen a need for having one at home, but now he wished he'd at least gotten a laptop for personal use. Who knew how long it would take to find out the information he needed?

As soon as he reached his desk, he flipped his computer on. While he waited for it to boot up, his boss approached him.

"Forget something?"

"No. I only needed to get a little research done."

"Oh . . . what kind?"

Luke knew that tone of voice. His boss assumed he was working on his forbidden story.

Not wanting to lie outright, he said, "I'm looking into the greeting card industry."

Partlow squinted, obviously suspicious. "Interesting. Mind if I look over your shoulder?"

Luke had no doubts about the lack of trust his boss had in him. What he didn't understand, was why Partlow got so upset whenever Luke mentioned his interest in the farm workers. However, this was his boss, and he was using a company computer. He'd never be able to explain to Partlow the sense of urgency he felt. He certainly didn't have time to purchase his own computer and sign up for Internet access. Time was running out.

"No problem. Is this subject something you think our readers would be interested in?"

Partlow sneered, his face contradicting his words. "I imagine they might if you put the proper spin on it."

Luke sat down and logged in. He typed the words "greeting card company" into the search engine. Dozens of companies came up. He had no idea there were so many. He had been familiar with two or three big name companies who advertised on TV, but he'd never turned a card over to see where it came from. Like most people, he made his purchases based on the cover and the verse inside.

One by one, Luke clicked on the different companies looking for the one that produced Aimee's cards. His boss must have finally got bored and wandered away.

After what seemed like hours, Luke finally found what he was looking for. The company handling Aimee's drawings was a subsidiary of a larger publishing house. He scrolled through every page on their site but didn't find any mention of her. However, he found a phone number for the publishing company. He wrote it down and looked at his watch. It had to be at least ten o'clock on the East Coast. He'd have to call them the next day.

He tucked the number in his pocket and turned off the computer. On his way out, his boss, who sat in front of his own computer called out, "Find what you were looking for?"

Again, the tone of voice caused concern to knife through Luke. Had Partlow been monitoring his web surfing? He tried to remember the sites he'd visited when looking for information about the farm workers. He remembered looking into immigration laws, and also the web site for the county Sheriff's office. No wonder his boss sounded like a prosecuting attorney. It could have looked to him as if Luke had deliberately disobeyed an order. Never mind that he'd done it on his own time. He'd used office equipment. Luke vowed to get his own laptop at his earliest opportunity.

He hoped the results of his search wouldn't come too late.

Early the next morning, before Luke left for work, he called the publishing house and asked to be connected to the greeting card division. They gave him a different phone number in a different city. Luke thanked them, hung up, and dialed the number. His stomach as tight as the skin on a drum, he waited for the person to answer who could give him information about Aimee. As he feared, they refused to release the information, citing privacy concerns.

Luke grabbed a bite to eat and left for the office. As soon as he got off work, he planned to scour the area near the orchards. She had to live nearby. He'd knock on every door in the county if necessary.

Partlow arrived at the office the same time Luke did. "Your column is due right after lunch." He stepped inside his office without another word.

Luke knew his days at that job were coming to a close. His boss no longer even pretended to be cordial. Normally he'd have till the end of the day to get his piece in.

Working on a column which benefited no one, seemed a waste of precious time. Time he should be using to find Aimee. The thought of her going through whatever situation she was in, and being all alone, killed his creativity, and in fact would certainly kill him if he didn't find her soon.

Getting information from her publisher had failed. He pulled one of her cards from his briefcase and again turned it over to look at the back. The trademark! Maybe he could trace her through that. He'd start looking as soon as he had a break.

Luke worked through lunch and turned his column in to the editor. Partlow decided to call an impromptu staff meeting right after, so Luke had no time to get back on the Internet. He could barely concentrate on what his boss was saying.

"So Luke. Any comments?"

Everybody at the table turned their attention toward him. *What had Partlow said?* It apparently had something to do with him.

"No comment? Then I'll expect to see your report on the basketball tournament on my desk first thing tomorrow."

Luke inwardly groaned. He'd been given a new assignment. One designed to bore him to death and keep him from his first priority. Covering sports news, as much as he enjoyed sports, was one step above being fired. Luke saw the staff sports writer had not appeared at the meeting. He'd probably been assigned to a hard news story . . . the kind Luke was dying to cover.

Everyone in the room, except him and his boss stood and filed out of the conference room.

Partlow approached him as he gathered his papers. Gone was the usual slap on the back. "Since you'll be covering the story tonight, you might as well take the rest of the day off."

Whatever you do, do as unto Christ. That meant giving respect to Partlow, as hard as it was.

"Thank you, sir. If you don't mind, I have a little more research to do on the greeting card story first."

"Is that really necessary? You may be busy covering the tournament for several days. I don't know when Jarvis is coming back to work."

So he was only filling in? "It won't take long."

"Make sure it doesn't. You don't want to take time away from familiarizing yourself with all the teams and players."

So much for taking the afternoon off.

"It won't."

"Good." Partlow sauntered away without another word.

Luke hurried to his desk and started another Internet search. He typed trademarks into the search engine and found a few sites that contained a trademark database. *Designs by Aimee.* He got a hit. There it was. With her full name and address! He printed out the page and snatched the sheet from the printer. Within minutes he was back in his vehicle.

Aimee arrived in Seattle after six hours of white knuckle driving through the mountains. The sheer volume of traffic in the big city, even so late at night, nearly made her want to go back. But that wasn't an option. Staying alive was priority one, so she exited the freeway and kept to the less traveled city streets.

It was far too late to check out rooms for rent, so she chose what looked to be an inexpensive motel away from the city center. The rate for a single shocked her. Back home, the amount would have fed a small family for several days. However her eyelids were so heavy, she dared not drive any further, and used the cash she'd gotten out of a Wenatchee ATM to check into a room.

She rose early the next morning, wondering how anyone got any sleep with all the noise from the trucks and buses rumbling down the streets. She made herself a cup of instant coffee, courtesy of the motel, and made plans for the rest of the day. She noted she had to check out of her room by eleven, so needed to get moving.

Getting settled was her next priority. Armed with a map and a newspaper, she made her way to a neighborhood near the Maria's hospital. After driving purposefully for over an hour, she finally found the address for the room for rent she'd marked in her paper. The neighborhood was old, but not decayed. She drove around the block, looking for a place to park. Relieved to note there were no unsavory types were hanging around the street corners, she decided to take the room if it were at all decent.

The woman who answered the doorbell spoke with a voice as harsh as her bleached blonde hair. "Do you have any references?"

Aimee wondered what information she dare give her. She didn't carry credit cards. The lease on the little house across the mountains was paid up until the end of the year to an absentee landlord. Not till the woman asked the questions, had Aimee considered how much of a non person she really was.

Luke would speak on her behalf, but he didn't know her whereabouts. And she had no intention of telling him before she was ready to see him face to face.

"I'm new to the city. I don't know anyone here yet."

The woman's eyes narrowed, making her look twice the age her hair and makeup attempted to mimic. "I insist on the rent being paid in advance. You can pay week to week if you need to, but if you're more than three days late with the rent, you're out."

"That sounds fine. Could I see the room?"

"Come on in, the woman growled."

Aimee followed her inside and up some stairs to the second floor. The house smelled of stale cooking oil and dog hair. She could hear a small dog yapping in a nearby room.

"Here it is." The woman shoved open a door and stood aside for Aimee to enter.

It was small, but Aimee was used to that. A twin bed stood in the corner, and was made up with a quilt old enough to share Aimee's birth year, but not old enough to qualify as an heirloom. A desk sat in front of the only window and a straight back chair sat next to it.

"I keep the desk here for college students. The boy who had this room before had to drop out of school and go home."

"A desk is good."

"Are you a student?"

How much should she tell? If somehow anyone traced her to this house, would her landlady protect her privacy?

"I'm a freelance artist. I work at home."

There's a phone jack behind the desk, but if you make any long distance calls, you'll have to use a calling card. No exceptions. I won't have anybody running up a phone bill."

"I understand."

"No parties, no loud music, no men in your room."

"That won't be a problem."

"You may use the kitchen, but I'd appreciate it if you didn't roam around my house. There are spaces in the refrigerator and cupboards market *renter*. You may use those spaces. No dirty dishes left in the sink. There's a vacuum in the upstairs hall closet. I hope you like to keep things clean."

"Yes I do."

"What happened to your face?"

Aimee hadn't expected anyone to be so direct. But she couldn't very well wear a ski mask every place she went. Whenever she'd gone out in public, to a store, or wherever, people saw her and averted their eyes.

"An accident."

The woman brushed Aimee's hair back from her face. "Oh boy. I guess we won't have to worry about a bunch of men swarming around here, now will we?"

Did the woman expect Aimee to flinch? She hadn't said anything that Aimee hadn't told herself over and over. She didn't care about a bunch of men. She only cared about one man--Luke. She hoped the circumstances of the last few weeks hadn't permanently ruined any chance she might have had with him.

Would he still be available when she was ready to resume the relationship?

"Are you going to take it, or not?"

"Yes. I think it will do fine." Aimee pulled out her wallet and gave the woman two week's rent. "What should I call you?"

"Blanche. Blanche Hemming."

"Thank you, Mrs. Hemming. I'll be a good tenant."

"You'd better. And it's "Miss" Hemming. No noose around my neck. I won't be no slave to any man."

Aimee excused herself to bring her things up to her room. Miss Hemming left a key to the front door, as well as a key to her room, on the desk. On her second trip downstairs, the landlady hollered out from somewhere downstairs, "Oh, I forgot to tell you. The bathroom is down the hall and to your right."

Aimee finished unloading her car, then stretched out on her bed, exhausted, and took a nap. Aimee's last thoughts before she drifted off were of Luke, telling her she had beautiful eyes.

CHAPTER TEN

Armed with Aimee's address, Luke drove up river to find her house. He traveled up and down the road several times before he found her house. The property sat back in some trees, very close to the bottom of Cherry Orchard Road. He was surprised to see her home was so small, even bearing a similarity to the farm workers' cabins up the hill.

He pulled into the driveway and parked. No lights shone through the windows, even though the sky was dark with storm clouds. The snow covered path to the front door, was disturbed, as if someone had walked there. Had the footprints been made by Aimee? A visitor? Or the mailman?

He sprinted up to the door and knocked. No answer. "Aimee!" He listened, hoping to hear footsteps inside, but the quiet stretched out like his lonely days waiting for her telephone call.

Luke didn't know what was worse, not knowing if she were safe, or thinking she was safe and she didn't want anything to do with him. He knocked again, harder. When that failed to get a response, he decided to walk around to the rear of the house. Even with the ground covered with snow, he could tell there had been a rather large well-tended garden in the back. That explained where she got the produce she shared with her friends.

He peered through the kitchen window. Nothing stirred inside. In fact, the room looked rather deserted. No dishes, appliances, or anything else on the counter. When he put his face right up next to the window, he could make out a teakettle sitting on a nineteen-fifty's era stove. Still, there was no sign of Aimee. Not her beautiful smile, her welcome laughter, nothing. It was as if she'd moved away.

How could she do this? Leave without a word? Hadn't their relationship meant anything at all to her? Was it fear that was keeping her from him? Even if she were hiding from the deputy, she could at least call him. The longer he stood there, the more the cold fear settled in his heart.

His shoulders slumped. He didn't know what to do next . . . where to look. He'd thought when he found her name and address, his search would be over, but it seemed like he was no closer than before.

He stepped off the back porch, and started back around the house. Next to the house, separated by only the path, stood a ramshackle garage. Footprints led to a side door. Had she left in a vehicle? He realized he didn't even know if she had one. He doubled back around the garage to see if there were tire tracks leading from the large door. There were none in the fresh snow. But someone had recently entered the building on foot. He went to the side door again. A single pane window, covered with a layer of grime, kept him from seeing inside. He tried wiping it off with his sleeve.

A noise came from within the building. A faint sound. Like a small animal rustling around. Luke put his hand on the doorknob. He turned the knob and pushed the door slightly with his other hand. A loud crash suddenly cut through the stillness. He shoved his way into the garage. The dark form of a man rushed toward him, nearly knocking him down. Luke grabbed the man's arm. The man growled, jerking his arm away. Luke hung on, not willing to let him escape. The intruder struggled to free himself from Luke's grip, but Luke hung on.

The man, who was several inches shorter than Luke, forced his way outside. Luke got a glimpse of his gray hair under his cap. Still, with Luke's advantage of youth, it was all he could do to hold the man.

"Let me go!"

Luke wasn't about to let the old man go till he found out his identity, and purpose for being at Aimee's house. He pushed the man to the side wall of the garage, and pinned him there, their faces inches from each other.

"Who are you?" Luke panted from the effort of holding the man.

"You first! Do you live here?"

"No, and you wouldn't be asking if *you* did. Tell me your name."

The man tried to pull away, but Luke had him trapped.

"Why are you hiding out in her garage?"

"Do you mean Aimee?"

"Yes, I mean Aimee. How do you know her? Where is she? What have you done with her?"

"I haven't done anything with her. I came looking for her and when I heard you pounding on the front door, I went into the garage to hide. You sounded angry."

"Likely story. It's more likely you're here to steal. Why else would you hide from me? Maybe we should call the police."

"Go ahead. I'll tell them how you assaulted me! I'll tell them I'm here to visit my daughter."

Luke nearly dropped his hold on the man. Aimee's father? "Do you have some proof?"

"I don't need any proof. We can wait till she gets home and she'll tell you."

Luke looked into the man's face. How could he discern any family resemblance when he didn't even know what Aimee looked like?

Luke's breathing returned to normal. The man stopped struggling, so he loosened his grip. Peering closely at the man's eyes, he noted the same color as Aimee's. However, lots of people had brown eyes. Everybody on the hill had brown eyes!

"Are you a friend of hers?"

"Yes. More than a friend, actually."

"Boyfriend? Husband?"

"You claim to be her father, and you don't even know if she's married?" Luke reached for the intruder again but the man jumped out of range.

"I haven't seen her for several years. I only recently learned where she lived after hearing about a fire on the evening news. It gave her first name as one of the witnesses and described her face. I had to find out for sure if it was my daughter."

Sure. Perhaps several people were looking for her. She'd been at the scene. She knew too much.

The man pulled out his wallet and thrust it toward Luke. "Here. Look inside--at my driver's license. You'll see my name is Jim McPherson."

Was he bluffing? No. Luke hadn't mentioned her last name. Luke took the wallet and opened it. He saw a driver's license displayed behind a clear plastic window. Sure enough, the man had been telling the truth. Even a crook wouldn't go so far as to get a phony driver's license to impersonate her father. He handed back the wallet.

"I'm sorry. I had no idea who you were. I thought you had harmed, or were intending to harm her."

"Why would you think that? Is she in some kind of danger?" Fear showed plainly on the man's face.

"Look, why don't we go have coffee someplace? We're not accomplishing anything standing out here in the cold."

"I left my car down at the end of the road. I didn't know if this was the right place or not."

"We'll take my car. I can bring you back later."

Luke took Jim to the same restaurant where he usually met Pastor Greg. Once they were seated across from each other, and the waitress had taken their order, a few moments of silence passed. Since it appeared Jim wanted Luke to start talking first, he might as well oblige.

"I haven't known your daughter a long time, but I do remember her saying she hadn't kept in touch with you."

"Did she tell you why?"

"I didn't pry. It seemed like a painful subject with her."

"That's my fault. I'm afraid I ran her off. At first, I thought good riddance, but as the months and years went by, I realized what a terrible mistake I made."

Luke couldn't imagine what being estranged from your family would be like. He'd been gone from home for a couple of years and still spoke to his parents on the phone at least once a week.

"Did you ever call her at all?"

"I didn't begin to know where to find her." I thought maybe she'd moved across the Mountains to Seattle, but on the other hand, I couldn't see her getting used to big city life."

"I know what you mean. Aimee seems perfectly content with working at home and visiting with the migrant farm workers."

"I'm not surprised she became a recluse. That's my fault too."

"How so?"

"Her scars. I told her they were the price she'd have to pay for killing her mother."

Killing her mother? Scars? Was there no end to the secrets Aimee had been keeping?

"I don't mean Aimee actually killed Betty. It was a horrible accident. One that could have been prevented if I'd only been home that night."

Luke's throat closed, thinking about how Aimee's father had accused and blamed her. "What happened?" He could barely get the words out.

"I was late getting home. Betty and Aimee had to get to choir practice. Normally I would drive them when the roads were icy. But they decided not to wait for me. Aimee was driving, and . . ." Jim's voice broke.

Luke waited for him to compose himself.

"She skidded off the road. The car rolled, pinning my Betty inside." He stopped again.

"You don't have to finish."

"Yes, I do. I've got to get this off my chest."

"I'm so sorry for your loss."

"It was Aimee's loss too. But in my anger and grief, I refused to see that."

"I'm sure the Lord will forgive you."

"I know He has. But I'm guessing Aimee hasn't, or she would have contacted me. And I don't blame her. I laid all the blame on her. She was alive and my wife died at the scene of the accident."

"You said Aimee has scars?"

"Inside and out. And it's my fault."

A beam of light shone on the puzzle of Aimee's illusiveness. Luke sympathized, but mostly he was angry. Did she have so little regard for their friendship that she wouldn't trust him?

"Do you have any idea why Aimee is so bitter against God?"

Jim averted his eyes. "Probably because I held God's judgment over her head. Those weeks after Betty's death, I lashed out at Aimee on a daily basis. Every time I saw the cuts and bruises on her face, I'd remind her how she was spared while her mother was dead. When her doctor advised plastic surgery to put her face back together, Aimee begged me for the money to get it done. I refused. I told her it was God's reminder to her every time she looked in the mirror."

Oh, Father. Your loving kindness never ends. I'm asking you now, to please heal Aimee's soul. Keep her safe and return her to us. Heal the breach between Aimee and her Dad and forgive Jim for the things he did to bring about their estrangement.

"Jim, are you sure you've asked God for forgiveness?"

"I'm very sure. The emptiness in my life nearly ruined me. I found myself merely going through the motions at work, home, even at church. I'd quit reading my Bible, quit praying, and no longer listened for His voice."

"What changed things for you?"

"I visited Betty's grave on the anniversary of her death. Some people only a few yards away were burying a loved one. Their father. They didn't lash out at God for taking him away. Instead, they sang, celebrated his life, and hugged each other. Though they grieved his absence, they found comfort in each other and their faith. I realized then that I had actually blamed God and had projected that blame onto my daughter."

Luke felt tears well up, as he watched Jim struggle through the account of that day. His heart nearly broke for Aimee.

Jim took a deep breath, and then continued. "I fell prostrate on the ground, unable to move because of my shame. God must have blinded those folks to what was going on, because not one of them came over to me to see if I were dead or alive. God had business to do with me right at that moment. I knew if I didn't seek forgiveness and set things straight, I might not get another chance."

"So you started to search for Aimee." It was a statement, not a question. Even talking about what had happened had helped Jim's recovery. God had brought them together. Luke was thankful.

"I suggest we work together to find Aimee. The authorities haven't arrested anyone yet for fire at the orchards. I'm concerned he may try to retaliate against her so she won't be able to identify him."

"I don't even know where to start."

"Let's go back to her house and look around. Maybe we'll find some clues there. Then I want to go talk to the people at the orchards."

"Do you mind my asking what your interest is in her?"

Could Luke admit, even to himself, he had fallen in love with a woman over the phone? He'd heard about pen pal romances, and Internet romances, but hadn't put much stock in those stories. Yet, God had put her in his life. Was it the answer to his prayer? That he could find a life partner before his thirtieth birthday? In light of the serious issues Aimee faced, Luke praying for a wife seemed frivolous. Still, didn't God care about his every need? Big *and* small?

"I care for your daughter very much. I'd like nothing better than to pursue a relationship with her. But we have a more urgent task at hand."

"Let's go then." Jim stood, throwing some bills on the table, and led the way out of the coffee shop.

Luke and Jim decided to stop at Aimee's home before heading to the orchards. Luke parked in front of the garage. They looked around, noting it didn't appear as if anyone had been there since they'd left. Both front and back doors were locked. They tried each of the windows, with no luck at finding a way in. They agreed it wouldn't be a good idea to break in. If Aimee did come back, she'd notice. They were worried about how frightened she'd be if faced with something like that.

Instead, they turned their attention to the garage. It held an assortment of well used garden tools. A small wheelbarrow. Shelves, holding various sized empty canning jars. By the way things were stored on the perimeter of the garage, they surmised it had indeed been used to park a car. The oil residue on the dirt floor, where the front of a car would sit, looked fairly recent. Leaning against the far wall, stood a bicycle. A large roomy basket was attached to the handlebars.

Luke looked the bike over carefully. The tires were full of air, and it looked well maintained. Aimee must have used it for local trips . . . perhaps even to visit the farm workers.

"It couldn't have been easy for her to pump that bicycle up the hill, even with the lower gears. I wonder why she didn't use her car."

"I'm surprised she had a car. She swore she'd never drive again."

"You have to admit, a bike has its limitations. It's way too far to Wenatchee to ride a bike. Especially in inclement weather."

Jim nodded and rustled through some other items in a small cupboard. "I don't see anything here that would help us."

"Me either. Let's head up the hill and talk to the people there."

Working as a team with Jim made Luke miss his own father. He also felt gratitude and thankfulness for the relationship he had with his own parents. He was looking forward to getting them out to visit. Hopefully, the arsonist would be behind bars by then. He looked forward to introducing them to Aimee.

They pulled into the area in front of the cabins just as the bus was unloading. Gabe got off the bus with his father which shocked Luke. Surely the boy hadn't gone to work with the men! He should be in school!

Gabe and Jim reached Juan's house at the same time Juan and Gabe did. Luke introduced the two men who shook hands.

"How is Maria?"

"She's still in the hospital. I called there from a pay phone and spoke with Carmelita."

"I'm glad her mother can stay with her."

"The hospital has special rooms for the mothers of the children. It costs us nothing."

103

"Will they be coming home soon?"

Juan's face fell. "Please come in. We can talk there." He opened the door and motioned Luke and Jim to enter.

Once inside, Juan moved to the kitchenette and poured water into a coffee pot. While he worked with the stove, Luke turned his attention toward Gabe. "You went with your father today?"

"Si." The boy lapsed into his native language, and would not meet Luke's gaze.

"Is it a school holiday?"

Gabe glanced toward his father, than looked down at the floor.

"Don't tell me you worked."

"Si, I work every day now."

Luke and Jim exchanged shocked looks. The boy couldn't have been more than ten or twelve years old.

Juan returned. "Sit. Please."

Gabe disappeared into a room at the rear of the cabin before Luke could question him more. He and Jim sat down.

"I'm sorry I have nothing to offer you to eat. We've been taking dinner with our friends."

"We didn't come here to eat. And we don't want to keep you."

Juan looked at him, with questions in his eyes.

"We're looking for Aimee. The one the children call, *Angel.*"

Juan's gaze darted toward the front door and back again. "She doesn't come here any more."

Jim shifted on the edge of his seat. "Where is she? I'm her father. We want to find her."

Juan looked at Jim with suspicion.

"She has no family. She told us *we* are her family."

Luke watched Juan grapple with fear and distrust. Luke had never been able to develop a close friendship with the man. He had the impression Carmelita came to church against his wishes, too. What would it take to overcome the man's distrust?

"We're here to help her. If you know where she is, you need to tell us."

Juan rose to his feet. "I'm sorry. I don't know anything." He walked to the door, making it clear he expected them to leave.

"Could we speak with Gabe before we go?"

"Gabe has to work on his studies." Juan opened the door. "I'll tell my wife you were here."

Luke reluctantly stood, and with Jim following, stepped outside on the porch. He pulled a business card from his pocket and scribbled his home number on the back. Handing it to Juan, he said, "Please call me if you see her. Or have her call me. Tell her it's important."

Juan took the card and went back inside, shutting the door. Luke and Jim looked at each other. "What do we do now?"

CHAPTER ELEVEN

Anxious to see Maria, Aimee, drove to the hospital. After several wrong turns, she finally found her room. Carmelita sat at her bedside, but rose when she saw Aimee. The women embraced.

"How is Maria?"

"She sleeps. And then she wakes up and cries. It is very bad when they change her bandages."

Aimee went to Maria's bedside. Bandages covered one side of her face and most of her beautiful black hair was gone.

"Maria, you have company." Carmelita had moved to the opposite side of the bed.

"Don't wake her. I'll be around for a long time."

"Don't you have to go home tonight?"

"No. I'm staying in the city for awhile. Is there anything I can bring you?"

"They give us everything here. And a lady even came and gave me a Bible in my own language."

So Maria believes in God. Aimee wasn't altogether surprised. Luke had told her she'd gone his church with him.

The little girl in the bed groaned.

"It's nearly time for her pain medication. Then they will change the bandages again. You won't want to be here for that."

Aimee cringed inside. Seeing the little girl in pain would break her heart, yet she wanted to be there for her and her mom. "I want to help however I can."

Maria whimpered and flung her arms out. Carmelita leaned over and pushed the call button to summon a nurse. "It will get much worse. Don't feel badly if you want to leave."

"I won't leave."

The little girl opened her eyes, but didn't focus on her mother or Aimee. Instead she stared at the ceiling, arching her back in agony. Aimee had never witnessed anything as heartbreaking. She felt Maria's pain. How did parents keep from breaking down while watching their child suffer?

A nurse arrived, her shoes barely making a whisper as she rushed in. She pulled a syringe from her pocket and injected something into Maria's IV line. *Oh, God. Please let her pain go away soon.*

Aimee no longer hesitated to pray for the little girl. God would listen to her prayers on behalf of a little one. It wasn't like praying for herself, which would have been selfish and presumptuous.

The nurse stood by till Maria quieted. The sympathy in her eyes as she stroked her patient's hand, said volumes about her dedication.

"She'll sleep again. You should use the time to get something to eat." She addressed Carmelita. "Perhaps your friend could take you to someplace away from the hospital."

"No! I can't leave my baby."

Aimee turned to the nurse. "Is there a cafeteria in the hospital? We could eat there, and if Maria needed us, we could be paged."

"Yes, there's one on the first floor. And there are loud speakers there just for that purpose."

They watched till Maria's breathing came evenly. She no longer thrashed around.

"Come on. I'll take you to eat."

"I don't have money to eat there. I usually eat the meals provided by the family guest unit."

"It's my treat. Besides, you need a change of scenery."

They took an elevator down to the main floor and followed the aroma of food till they found the dining area. After filling their plates from the buffet, they sat at a small table overlooking a courtyard. Instead of the white sparkling snow they had at home, drizzling rain slapped against the window. Aimee tried to ignore the gloomy weather and encouraged Carmelita to make small talk as they ate. The conversation always turned back to Maria.

"How long till Maria can go home?"

It may be a few weeks. Before Christmas though. They want us to come back for an operation, but there is no money for that. The burn foundation only pays for the time till she'd healed."

"What kind of operation?"

"I don't know what it's called. They say it will make her face look normal again. If she doesn't get this, her face will always look bad from the burns."

Aimee's heart nearly stopped. The physical pain was severe enough, but the emotional suffering Maria would have to endure shattered her. She knew exactly what was in store for the little girl. The only difference between Maria and Aimee's injuries was that Maria would have both her parents there for her.

"When do you have to make your decision?"

"They want to operate soon. Maybe right after Christmas. But even with both Gabe and Juan working, we won't have enough money."

"Gabe is working now?"

"He wants to help."

"But he's not old enough to work."

Carmelita's face flushed. "He lied about his age."

"Don't give up yet. There has to be a way."

Carmelita pushed her plate away and stood. "I have to get back."

Aimee rose and hugged her. "I'll return tomorrow."

"Thank you." Carmelita's dark eyes filled with tears. "It's nice to have somebody to talk to. I miss my Juan."

The two women returned to find Maria still sleeping. "Perhaps you should take a nap too, Carmelita. I'll come back tomorrow."

The drive back to the rooming house was difficult, due to Aimee's unshed tears. When she arrived, she pulled up to the curb in front and turned off the ignition. *God, I know we haven't been close the last few years, but please, please help Maria get well. I'll do whatever You ask if You make her well again.* Resting her head and arms on the steering wheel, she gave in and cried till there were no tears left.

A tap on the window made her sit up. "It's me. Blanche. Open the door."

Aimee wiped her eyes with her sleeve and rolled down the window. "What is it, Ms. Hemming? Is something wrong?"

"It's *Blanche,* and I should be asking you the same thing. Why are you sitting out here bawling your head off?"

"I've just come from the hospital where a little girl I know is trying to heal from some bad burns on her face."

"Well, there's nothing you can do sitting out here. Come on in. I'll fix a pot of tea and we can talk."

Aimee didn't feel much like talking to a perfect stranger, but maybe Blanche could help her sort out her feelings. She followed her landlady into the house. Blanche seated Aimee at her kitchen table and after putting the teapot on, sat across from her.

"Now tell me all about it."

"I love that little girl. I know what lies ahead of her and I can hardly stand it."

"Sounds like there's not much you can do to help."

"But there is. I have money saved up. I want to use it for Maria's surgery. Then she won't have to go through life hating her own face."

Blanche reached across the table and took Aimee's hand. "You mean like you." She said it as a statement, not a question.

"Yes." Aimee's throat constricted, threatening to cut off her air.

"So what's the problem?"

Aimee looked deep within herself. Giving up on her dream of being with Luke tore her heart to shreds. But no other solution existed.

***

Luke asked Jim to stay at his place. It didn't make sense for him to stay at a motel, and the drive back and forth from Wenatchee to Yakima, where the other man lived, didn't make sense. Jim had taken vacation time off, so there was nothing pressing for him to do at his home.

It was good to have someone to vent to. Jim seemed as frustrated as Luke. All they'd uncovered so far were dead ends. Knowing someone else might be looking for her too, gave them a sense of urgency neither one knew how to handle. They prayed. Together, and individually. Luke prayed constantly in his heart as they considered every possibility.

"There was no sign of a break-in. And her car is gone. I think that's a good sign. It shows she knows she's in danger, and is hiding." Jim tried to comfort Luke with his words, but sounded as if he were trying to convince himself as well.

"But why hasn't she called me? Surely she knows I'd help her."

"You said you've never actually seen her face? Perhaps she's still intent on hiding that from you."

"It's her heart I care for. I wish I would have told her. But how could I? I didn't have a clue this would happen."

"We need to trust God. He led me to her and to you. He knows where she is. He'll bring us through this."

110

"Do you think we should report her as missing? I haven't known who to trust, but surely the more people who know, the less likely it is that the arsonist would harm her."

"Not yet. I think we need to trust Aimee. Look at how well she's kept hidden from me."

"Then what should we do next?"

"The key has to be with the farm workers. Look how Juan shut us down when we mentioned her. Isn't she as likely to contact him as you? She'll want to know how Maria is doing."

Luke pondered what Jim had said. The one constant he knew about Aimee, was her love for those people.

"I don't think questioning them again will help."

"Then we'll watch and wait. And pray."

***

After her visit with Maria and her mother, Aimee knew it was time to call Luke. To hear his voice one more time. He picked up on the first ring.

"This is Aimee."

"Aimee! Where are you? We've been looking everywhere for you!"

"We?"

"Those of us who care about you. Give me your location. I'll come to you."

"I'm calling long distance."

"From where? Are you OK?"

Aimee's spirit soared to know Luke cared for her. However, she knew the knowledge would no longer benefit her. "I'm fine. I called to see if there's been an arrest in the arson case."

"Not yet, but I'm determined to prove who did it. It would help if you would come back and give a statement to the police."

"I mailed my statement to the arson investigator."

"But if there's a trial, they'll need your testimony."

"Isn't there any other way? It would be a long way for me to travel."

"Aimee, I can't believe you wouldn't jump at the chance to put that creep behind bars. Don't you remember what happened to Maria?"

"Of course I remember! How could I forget? I was there when they took her away in the ambulance." Aimee's voice broke. She hoped Luke hadn't noticed how close to tears she was.

"I'm sorry. That was uncalled for on my part. I know how much you love her."

She's not the only one I love.

"There's someone else who has been searching for you."

"I know. The deputy."

"No. Your father."

"How did--" Aimee slapped her hand over her mouth to hold back a sob.

"How did he find you?"

From the TV account of the fire. We met when we both went to your house at the same time."

"You know where I lived?"

"You say it in past tense. Does this mean you don't plan on coming back?"

"I can't." *Especially now.*

"At least give me your new address and phone number so your father can contact you."

"Why would he want to?"

"Aimee." The gentleness in Luke's voice nearly ripped her heart in half. "Things have changed. But he needs to tell you himself."

"Tell him I'll call him then." It was easier for Aimee to agree, than to argue with Luke about her father.

"Aimee, won't you please come back? You don't have to hide from me. I know everything."

Her father must have told Luke how she killed her mother. He'd told him what a hideous excuse for a human she was.

"I have to go."

"Wait!" Luke's plea nearly made her come unglued. "Will you call me again?"

"Goodbye, Luke." Aimee replaced the receiver. It had been a mistake to call Luke. Hearing his voice only made her decision harder.

Aimee pulled her bankbook out of her purse. The balance would be enough to insure Maria's surgery with a little left over for the help her family start over in a new place. Aimee's dreams were insignificant in comparison. No little girl, especially one as sweet as Maria, should have to go through life scarred.

***

Luke slammed his fist on the table. "I thought she cared about me! I thought she would help me put that crook away! Is her vanity so incredibly important she can't think of anyone but herself?

Jim walked over and gripped Luke's shoulder. "I know, son. It hurts. But don't blame Aimee. The entire thing is my fault."

"She didn't even give me a chance to explain. The minute she thought I was getting too close, she ran. Just like she ran from you."

"She isn't running from us. She's running from the pain."

"I don't know how to overcome that. She needs something beyond what I can give her."

"Give her your love and forgiveness. God will do the rest. Look at me? Do you think I deserve to be forgiven after what I've done to her? Yet the Lord has forgiven me. He's letting me start over with a clean slate. If He'll do it for me, He'll do it for anyone."

"I don't know what to say. I thought I might have a future with your daughter. We clicked . . . the very first time we spoke. I knew there was something special about her. We were beginning to care about each other. And all this time, she never intended to let me close enough to even see her face!"

Luke turned and stormed from the apartment.

Later that evening, after he'd calmed down, Luke parked his van in Aimee's garage. He and Jim got out. "Dressing in dark clothing isn't going to help a lot with all the snow on the ground. We might as well drive up the hill with the radio blaring.

"I didn't think of it either. We'll just have to duck out of sight if we hear someone coming.

"Some sleuths we make, huh?"

They headed up the hill on foot. A clear sky and full moon made it easy to keep their footing and not wander off into a ditch. Both sides of the road were lined with fruit trees, their leaves dropped long ago. Each time they heard the sound of a motor, they stopped and listened. "Noises travel a long way during a night like this."

"Let's just keep going. There are plenty of places to jump off the road if we see headlights approaching"

"I hope we don't have to. At my age, I'd probably break a leg.

"Luke chuckled at the older man's comment. He had a hard time keeping up with him.

"I don't know how your daughter made this trip so often."

"Do you think she drove?"

"I don't think so. I never saw evidence of her coming up here by car."

"She used the bike, then. When she was a teen, before she got her driver's license, she rode a bike everywhere. Even when her mother or I offered to drive her. She said she loved being out in the sun. Of course we insisted on driving her during the winter."

"Sounds like you were good parents."

"We were a very close-knit family. I must have been crazy to carry on the way I did after Betty died."

"I didn't mean for you to turn my words into a guilt trip."

"I know. But I'll always have regrets."

Luke spotted the cabins in the distance. "We're almost there."

"Good. Let's hope we have good luck tonight. I don't know how many times my old legs will take walking up this hill."

Luke led Jim around behind Juan's burnt out cabin. As he'd hoped, the dogs had been taken inside for the night. If they started barking, it would ruin everything.

They hunkered down inside a woodshed, grateful for the down jackets and pocket warmers they'd brought. Every so often, one of them would stand and stretch, looking around for anything . . . or anyone . . . out of place. The minutes turned into hours and finally they called it a night. Nobody would be coming once dawn approached.

Every night that week, they followed the same routine. Luke used the time to pray for Aimee. He knew when he saw Jim moving his lips, that he was doing the same.

Early Saturday morning, they returned to the apartment and sat at Luke's kitchen table sipping hot coffee.

"Do you think I should go up there as usual to pick up anyone wanting to go to church?"

"They're expecting you to. You don't want to give anyone the impressions you're intimidated."

"After all, it could have been my visits that incited the deputy to retaliate."

"You don't know that for sure."

"Let's take a nap, and I'll give Mitch a call this afternoon."

***

Luke woke later in the day. He got some cold cuts and cheese out of the fridge. When he heard Jim stir in the spare room, he figured he'd be hungry too. He was digging around looking for the dill pickles when the phone rang.

Will I ever quit rushing to the phone because it could be Aimee?

"Hello?"

"Luke. I need you to cover a game again tonight."

Partlow and his rotten timing.

"I've tried to reach you last night, but you must have been out."

"You didn't leave a message."

Because I didn't want you to have time to think up an excuse to say no."

"I don't need to dream up an excuse. I have company here from out of town. Working tonight, on my day off, is out of the question."

"You're making it difficult for me to continue to value your contribution to the paper."

Luke gritted his teeth. Although the relationship with his boss had started out well, it had been far from good ever since he'd brought up the issue of migrant farm workers. Now it seemed as if Partlow went out of his way to make his job unpleasant.

"I'm sorry you feel that way. I've filled in for Jarvis several times already as well as provided you with a daily column. I don't think it's unreasonable to expect to not work on my days off."

"I know you've been working from home and not showing up to the office. What are you really up to?"

116

"I've attended every staff meeting. You've never objected before if I worked from home, as long as I met my deadlines."

"Working at home is reserved for employees who have proven their loyalty to the paper."

"Meaning?"

"I don't think I need to explain it to you again."

"With all due respect, sir, what I do on my own time, doesn't affect the paper, and is my decision to make."

"Young man, you've just made the wrong decision. I want to see you in my office Monday morning to discuss your severance package"

"You're firing me?"

"You've given me no choice. If you decide to come around to our way of thinking by Monday morning, we can discuss it, but I wouldn't hold out much hope for your future with this paper."

CHAPTER TWELVE

Sunday morning, Luke woke up discouraged. Another long unproductive night made him question his decision of not covering the game for the paper.

Later, Jim came with Luke to pick up anyone wanting to go to church. This time, they didn't bring a whole parade of cars, just Luke's van and Mitch's Wagoneer. They pulled up in front of the cabin Juan and Gabe lived in since the fire. Gabe came out and Luke was pleased to see a half dozen other children came out as well. Gabe hopped in the back of the van with two of his friends. When it looked like no one else was coming, Jim slid the back door shut.

"Wait!" Gabe wrenched the door open. "Wait for Papa." Jim and Luke exchanged glances, both understanding they'd passed a landmark of sorts.

Jim squeezed in with the kids, leaving the front seat open for Juan.

Juan came out, walking directly to the van. Luke motioned him inside.

"I told Carmelita I'd come this morning. To pray for Maria."

"You know the Lord hears your prayers wherever you are," Luke said. "Not that I'm not very glad you're coming. So you've spoken to her then?"

"I call from the pay phone down at the store. I can't afford to call every day, but I do as often as I can."

Luke made a mental note to get some calling cards for the other man.

"I'll bet you miss your family. Is Maria doing well?"

"She is healing. Very slowly."

"You are so blessed that God spared her life."

"I know. This is why I must go to church and pray. To give thanks."

Luke's heart swelled with thanksgiving as well. He had doubted Juan would ever come with them. Yet there he was, riding along like it was a weekly thing. Given his earlier misgivings, he must have overcome his cynicism about church when his daughter was injured. Finally something good had happened.

Not wanting to give Juan any reason to feel like an outsider, he stuck close to him when they arrived at church.

***

Luke was pleased with the way the morning's service went. Juan had tensed when has saw the size of the church. However, everyone made him feel so welcome, he soon relaxed. The children who were first time visitors appeared to have enjoyed it as well. Luke looked forward to the following week. He'd round up more drivers and cars. He had no doubts this time they'd need them.

Luke and Jim kept their eyes open for the deputy when they took everyone home. There was no patrol car in sight. Had the cop given up his surveillance? Or had he only been working in another part of the county? There was a plain brown sedan coming down the road as they ascended the hill, but that was all.

Luke hadn't told Juan they had been watching their homes every night. No use alarming him. Plus, the less people who knew, the better. The only ones who knew were Mitch, and Pastor Greg. Mitch had warned him to be careful. He'd pointed out Luke and Jim weren't exactly trained as spies.

The danger to them was minimal compared to the threat to the helpless families. Then there was Aimee. Until he had her safe in his sight, he wouldn't quit worrying about her. She'd already endured enough tragedy in her life. He'd give his life to protect her. But how could he, when he didn't even know where she was?

119

Jim called his employer and left a message he would be taking an additional week off. Then he went off for his usual nap.

Luke tried lying down, but couldn't stop his racing thoughts long enough to relax for a nap. He finally gave up and went into the living room to read the Sunday paper.

When the phone rang, he jumped up, the paper falling to the floor around his feet. It might be Aimee. Her distinctive voice filled his dreams every time he did manage to grab a little sleep.

"Hello?"

"Son!"

"Dad! It's good to hear your voice. You must be doing better."

"The doctors couldn't be happier. I want to thank you for keeping in close touch with your mother while I was in the hospital."

"I still think I should have been there."

"No need for that. The doc says I'll be fit as a fiddle in another week. What would you say about your mother and me coming out to visit? Your thirtieth birthday and Christmas are coming up."

"That would be great! In fact, I've been planning something for you. A kind of combination "glad you are well," and Christmas gift."

"What's that?"

"There's a bed and breakfast up near Leavenworth with a hot tub, sleigh rides, and a four star restaurant attached. It's supposed to be very romantic. It would be a good place for you and Mother to kick back and relax."

"Sounds like just the thing she needs after all her fretting over me. How does the week before Christmas sound? We'll fly into SeaTac and rent a car."

"Are you sure you don't want me to come over and pick you up? Should you be driving?"

"I'll be fine. And we'll enjoy seeing the sights on the way over."

"OK, let me know what day you're arriving, and I'll make your room reservations. And Dad, there's someone I'd like you to meet."

"A young woman? Your mother will be tickled to hear that."

"I don't know if she'll be around, but yes, her name is Aimee McPherson. She designs greeting cards. Designs by Aimee. Mother has probably seen them in the Christian bookstores."

"We're looking forward to it."

"I am too." If he could get her to overcome her fear of being seen. But God was working on that.

**

Sunday night's temperature was the coldest Luke and Jim had encountered since they began watching the cabins. The wind whipped down the canyons, erasing the footprints they'd made in the powdery snow. Thinsulate underwear and hand warmers helped make their task bearable.

Lights in the windows signified some of the cabin inhabitants were still up, Juan and Gabe's place included. Two hours went by. One by one the lights were extinguished. All except Juan's cabin. As the temperature dropped, Luke was tempted to tap on Juan's door, but then he'd be faced with explaining what he and Jim were doing up there so late.

Jim tapped a button on his watch, illuminating the time. "He's up late tonight."

"Maybe it's Gabe doing his school work. He's still trying to work in the orchards and keep up with his studies. I wish I could prevent him from working, but their sense of family responsibility is so strong, I know I'd have no luck."

"You may be underestimating the respect they have for you. Why don't you try and talk to Juan? The boy can't be earning that much. Maybe we could take up a collection at church. I know I'd donate to help their family."

Luke smiled at Jim, even thought the other man couldn't see him in the dark. Their growing friendship comforted Luke. It had come out of nowhere, but was destined to last a lifetime. It didn't hurt that they both loved Aimee.

"Did you hear that?"

Luke listened, holding his breath. The distant sound of a car motor broke the silence. "Yeah. It sound's like it's coming closer."

They hunkered down lower in their hiding place, ears alert. Soon they saw headlights reflected on the trees.

"It's coming here." Luke's breathing quickened. Was this who they'd been waiting for?" They'd know soon.

The car turned into the area in front of the cabins. Luke and Jim ducked down before the headlights exposed them.

The vehicle stopped behind the old school bus. Luke wished he could stop his heart from pounding. Whoever was sitting out there could probably hear it. A click, then a faint squeak of a car door. Jim tapped him on the arm. Luke nodded his head.

The expected sound of footsteps didn't reach their ears. Whoever had driven up was either standing and looking around, or the quietest walker Luke had ever known. They couldn't have been discovered. They were too well hidden, even if someone had an advantage of night vision goggles. He doubted if their quarry was that high tech, but one never knew.

A tap on a door sounded from their right. Juan's door. Luke peeked around the corner. Light poured from the open door onto the snow outside.

"Get that mongrel away from me!" The man silhouetted in the door gave Gabe's dog a kick.

"He wants to go outside."

"Then see that he stays outside."

The man entered the cabin, closing the door behind him.

"Oh great. Now we have a dog to worry about," Jim whispered.

"He doesn't bite, but he's liable to put up a fuss when he discovers us."

"Then we'll have to distract him." Jim pulled a sandwich from his pocket. "All we have to do is lure him over here and give him my ham and cheese on rye."

"Let's hope it works."

Somewhere on the other side of the Cabin, a cat screeched in anger. They waited for the dog to find them but it must have gone in the opposite direction, chasing more interesting prey.

"Did you get a look at the man's face?"

"I didn't have to. Take a look at the car."

"Well look at the light bar on top. Do you suppose this is an official visit?"

"There's only one way to find out. Come on." Luke rose to his feet and Jim did the same.

"Keep your sandwich handy. Better give the dog a little piece at a time if he comes toward us. Then he'll stay quiet longer in case we have to get away."

"Gotcha."

They crept over to Juan's place, keeping their bodies flat against the walls of the other cabins. The dog still hadn't caught on to their presence. Evidently it was off following a rabbit scent. Luke hoped the hare ran off a good distance away and in the opposite direction.

They eased up to one of the windows. They couldn't see inside, but the cabins were so poorly constructed, and lacking in insulation, they could hear a little of what went on inside. Luke uncovered his ears, straining to make out the conversation.

"You got my money?"

"Most of it."

"I warned you, didn't I, what would happen if you didn't come up with all of it. How much are you short?"

"Only about fifty dollars. I had to buy a bus ticket for Carmelita to go to the hospital with our little girl."

"You don't seem to understand. When I told you how much money I wanted to keep things safe around here, I didn't say anything about needing half the money. You were already behind in your payments, Juan. Maybe next time all these shacks will burn down. What will you do then?"

"Please. My little girl was burned bad in the fire--"

"Another thing. You've been getting buddy buddy with that newspaper guy. What is he snoopin' around here for anyway?"

"He takes our people to church."

"It's not any do-gooders from any church that keeps your family safe. And that friend of yours isn't going to do you any good if I contact immigration."

"But I have my green card."

"Does everyone in this dump have one? What if I say they've been forged? Nobody will believe you."

"I'll get the money. Come back tomorrow."

A thud, followed by a piece of furniture being overturned was the next thing Luke heard. Then from behind him, another sound.

GRRRRRR

"QUICK! Where's the sandwich?"

"I'm looking for it!"

The dog came closer, a growl deep in its throat. Then it barked. Three times in a row.

"Jim, get out of here. That jerk inside doesn't know you. Go call the cops. I think we've got all we need. I'll stay here."

Jim found the sandwich and dropped it at Luke's feet. The dog went right for the food. "What about you? You're liable to be caught."

"Don't worry about me. I'll keep him busy so you won't be followed. Now get going!"

Jim took off running just as the door to Juan's cabin opened.

"Who's there!"

Luke slid around to the back of the cabin, but the dog followed him, whining.

Footsteps bounded down the porch steps. Someone was coming around after him. He had a large flashlight. And if he was the man who drove up in the patrol car, he also had a gun.

Lord, help me. Luke uttered the most basic prayer a man could.

"Come on out and put your hands where I can see them!"

Luke was trapped. No matter which way he went, he'd be toast.

"Do it now!"

Luke gave up and took a calming breath. *Jim should be a part of the way down the hill by now.* The dog jumped up on him, his forepaws on his chest. He pushed the dog away.

"OK, Buddy. Come the rest of the way out. I've got you covered."

Even though the beam of the flashlight nearly blinded him, Luke could see the gun in the man's other hand.

"It's you!"

"What's the problem, officer?"

"Don't get cute. Turn around and put your hands on the wall."

Luke stood his ground. "I don't think you want to do this. Harassment of a citizen will be added to your other charges."

"What are you yammering about?" growled the deputy.

"You're the one going to jail. We've got all the evidence we need."

"Oh yeah? You and who else?"

"My friend, who is probably calling the police right now."

The deputy glanced around, and then took a step toward him. "You're all talk."

"We've got proof you've been extorting money from these people. We've got proof you started both fires. Is that enough to put you away?" Luke was glad the darkness partially covered him. His hands shook like crazy and it wasn't from the cold.

The cop swung his flashlight, grazing Luke on the cheek. He'd seen it coming in time to step back. The dog snarled, this time at the deputy. Apparently a ham and cheese sandwich bought a lot of loyalty.

"If you know what's good for you, you'll get out of here and keep your mouth shut."

"Or what? You'll arrest me? I haven't done anything wrong."

"Your boss is a good friend of mine. All I have to do is make a phone call and your job is history."

"Sorry fella, but somebody beat you to it. I no longer work for your friend."

The deputy turned and headed toward his patrol car. The dog went after him, tearing at his pant legs.

"Get him off me or I'll shoot the mangy thing!"

Juan's voice rang out, calling the dog back. The dog reluctantly let go, and with its head hanging, meandered toward the porch.

126

The deputy walked away. He holstered his gun, and for the first time since the confrontation began, Luke breathed easy.

The patrol car started, turned around, and left.

"You shouldn't have done that."

"It's OK Juan. He won't be coming back. He's going to lose his job and will probably go to jail for quite a while."

"You don't know him. He'll find a way to get back. None of us will be safe."

"I promise you. He won't bother you any more. With the testimony Jim and I will give the police, he'll probably be arrested this very night."

"It's your word against his." There was no mistaking the fear in Juan's voice.

"If he gets out of jail, I'll stay here with you every night till he's put away for good."

"No! I don't want you here! Don't ever come here again. You've brought more trouble for us. I want you to leave us alone. Leave here now and don't come back!"

Juan's tone had changed from fear to extreme anger. There wasn't going to be a thing Luke could say to change his mind.

Had he turned the man against him forever?

What now, Lord?

CHAPTER THIRTEEN

Luke had plenty of free time on his hands since he'd lost his job. He dropped his resume off at the other newspaper offices in Wenatchee. However, he was in no big hurry to start work again. He'd had vacation time coming and that, plus his savings, would tide him over for a while.

He spent a lot of time checking Aimee's house. Nobody seemed to be checking her mailbox, but as near as he could tell, only a stray piece of bulk mail got put in there. However, he had God's peace regarding her safety.

It didn't hurt that the deputy was still in jail. Luke had gotten well acquainted with the prosecutor on the case. Since the charges ran from extortion, to arson, to attempted murder, and the man had the means to skip the state, the court had denied bail.

***

Aimee dare not call Luke again. It would only upset both of them. There was no way she'd ever ask him to wait for a couple more years, or however long it would take to build her bank account back up again.

He was so decent and kind, he'd tell her that the scars wouldn't matter. He might even *feel* that way at first. But once the newness of things wore off, he'd begin comparing her with other, *beautiful*, women. She wouldn't be able to stand the pity in everyone's eyes. The pity for Luke, who would be stuck with her due to his compulsive promises.

The loneliness of her self-imposed seclusion ate at her confidence, and even her creativity. But she had to suck it up. Working had always been good therapy. Not to mention, a way to keep food on the table.

Without Luke in her life, though, she didn't know how to get through the days with nobody to share things with. Not one other person cared about the same things they did.

Daddy. Luke had said her father wanted to speak to her. That things with him had changed. She wanted to believe it. She desperately wanted to erase all the years of being his enemy. Aimee closed her eyes, remembering the good times she'd enjoyed with her parents. When her father laughed and teased, and gave her hugs. Before he became an angry bitter man.

Aimee still had her Dad's phone number imprinted in her memory. What if she called him? If he started in on her again, she could always hang up. *I'm afraid. If he rejects me this time, it will be the last time I ever hear his voice. I won't put myself through that again.*

She reached for the phone, and then pulled her hand back. Her dreams of a life with Luke had burnt up with the cabin on the hill. Did she have the strength to risk losing her dad all over again too? Yet, if she could only hear his voice. Maybe she could call and try and discern his mood before she spoke.

I'm so lonely. There's not a single person who cares whether I live or die. She buried her face in her hands. She wouldn't cry. She refused to give in to her self-pity. Aimee pressed her lips together. She could start over again. Lots of people who weren't as young as she was, started over with nothing. She still had her health. She had her talent. Her contract. She could do it. Besides, she wouldn't change a thing. If given the choice, she'd give it all up to help Maria again.

If she regretted anything, it was disappointing Luke. He'd tried so hard to be a friend to her. To lead her back to his God. She'd thought a lot about the things he'd told her. The truth was, if God had spent as much time punishing her as she'd imagined, she'd be rotting in a grave by now. Wasn't she equally as guilty? If God had turned his back on her, she'd turned away first. She let her guilt take over every aspect of her life. Her dad's anger only compounded her problem.

Luke spoke of God's love all the time. If she had listened closer, maybe she could have come to believe again, too. Isn't that what she really wanted? If she couldn't have Luke, she'd at least have a shot of having some peace about it.

Aimee pulled her sketchpad toward her. She had a binder full of likenesses of Luke, beginning with the first one she'd drawn the day they slid down the hill on Gabe's cardboard sled. Since then, she'd find herself doodling as she daydreamed. Luke's smile, dimples on each side of his mouth. His forehead, and the way his hair fell over it. His hands. Folded in prayer, holding a Bible. It was so much part of who he was.

She'd trusted him. Respected him. And he had told her it was Ok to call her dad.

She drew the outline of a man's head, and then filled in eyes, nose, and mouth. The eyebrows were next. Where to put the hairline? Her dad had been thinning a little in front when she'd seen him last. Had he lost more hair by now?

Aimee closed the tablet. She'd put it off long enough. She pulled out her calling card punched in the numbers.

Her dad answered the phone on the third ring. "Hello."

Aimee's throat closed. The muscles in her jaw tightened until she wanted to scream with the pain.

"Hello?"

It was her dad. Her dad.

"It's . . . it's me."

"Aimee? Darlin'? I prayed you would call. Can you come home? There's so much I need to tell you. So much I need to make up for."

She didn't know how to answer.

"Aimee, just listen, for only a moment, I have something to tell you."

A sob caught in Aimee's throat. *Could* she listen for just one minute? She had to take a chance it wouldn't all start up again. For Luke. So he'd know she wasn't a totally terrible person. There was no doubt Luke would look for her and call her father in the process."

"Aimee? Are you there?"

"Yes." One word was all she could get out. She didn't want to cry. If she did, she might never be able to stop.

"God didn't turn his back on you. I did. I was wrong. Could you please forgive me?"

The words she had longed for. She couldn't even speak.

"Sweetheart, I don't blame you if you never forgave me. But could you at least give me a chance to make it up to you?"

Could he? What had she lost? Nearly six years? Six years of torture?

"At least let God back into your life. He loves you and won't ever let you down like I have."

"That's what Luke would say." She finally found the words to answer.

"If you can't trust me, trust Luke. He loves you."

Luke loves me? It wasn't possible. Perhaps her father didn't know she'd brushed him off the last time they spoke. Her emotions choked her, making it impossible to respond right away.

"How do you know so much about Luke?"

"We've become close friends. He's been searching everywhere for you. I know he's going to your house every day to see if you've been there."

"I'm not going back there, Daddy."

"Why not?"

"There's nothing for me there any longer. Did you know Luke has never seen my . . . my hideous face? No man wants a deformed monster for a friend."

"He cares for you much more than a friend. He cares like a man loves a woman."

"How can that be possible?"

"He says God picked you out for him. Under those circumstances, do you really think he cares how you look?"

Could it be true?

"Besides, your scars can be removed. I'll pay for whatever surgeries you need."

"It's an awful lot of money, Daddy."

"I don't care how much it takes. Don't you know I'd sell everything I own to help you?"

"But I killed mother." Tears rolled off her cheeks. She tried to wipe them away as she choked back a sob.

"It was an accident. I always knew that. I'll never forgive myself for blaming you. Oh, girl. If I could only be with you now to hug you."

Aimee wanted to believe her father. She wanted to erase all his ugly words from her memory. Could she really hope for reconciliation?

"I don't know if I'm ready to see you yet."

"That gives me hope that the day will come. I'll continue to pray for you every day. Call me when you're ready. I know I'm asking a lot of you right now."

"OK, I will."

"Will you call Luke?"

"I can't. I can't face him."

"You'll find the strength. I know you will. You're a strong woman, just like your mother was."

Aimee could no longer hold back the sobs. She broke the connection. A few moments later she dropped to her knees next to her bed. Maybe God would listen to her now.

***

"Hi Jim, It's me." Luke couldn't wait to tell Jim the news.

"You sound chipper this evening. What's up?"

"I just got off the phone with the prosecutor. It seems our friend, the deputy, has agreed to plead guilty to two counts of arson, and extortion, if . . . the attempted murder

132

charges are dropped. Needless to say, he no longer has a job, nor will he ever work for law enforcement again."

"But what about jail time?"

"Oh, he's going to jail. And for a long time. Plus he has to make restitution, and pay back all the money he took from Juan, plus interest."

"So our friends at the orchards will be safe for awhile. That is good news."

"And guess what, my former boss is his wife's brother! That explains a lot about the treatment I got at work. However, the police are positive Partlow knew nothing about his brother-in-law's criminal activities."

"Does anyone know why the deputy had it in for those folks?"

"Apparently money was the motive. He wanted to live the lifestyle his wife's family was used to. The fires were his way of keeping the pressure on Juan. Also, I learned they were already investigating him. Seems he was buying things no deputy could afford on his salary. Juan's little community wasn't the only one he'd extorted money from. And then there were the complaints from the public. He'd roughed up a number of people."

"So does this mean you'll be getting your old job back?"

"Partlow did call me and apologize, but I think we both knew his paper and my interests are not a good fit."

"What are you going to do?"

"I'm not sure, but I'll make a decision by Christmas."

"That's only a week away."

"I know. My folks are coming out to spend the holidays with me. Hey, why don't you come up and meet them? I know you would really take to each other."

"I'll consider it." Jim paused as if pondering what to say.

"You'd better do more than consider it, friend."

"Aimee called me."

Oh, thank you Lord! "How did it go?"

"I think there's a chance we can put things back together."

"Where is she? Did she say?"

"No, but my caller ID indicated a Seattle area code. I'm assuming she's there to give emotional support to Maria and her mother."

"So you have her number, then? Give it to me."

"Luke, I'm sorry, but she doesn't want to talk to you."

Luke's heart fell. He hadn't wanted to hear that. "Did she say why?"

"Aimee still has a lot of issues with her appearance. Plus, she has to find her faith again. I don't know how long it will take to resolve that. In the meantime, I'm afraid talking to you would only upset her."

"She'll change her mind. As soon as she comes home, I'll sit down with her and we can talk these things through. I love her, you know."

"I know. But she's not *coming* back."

"You mean, not before Maria is released from the hospital."

"Not ever. She was adamant about that."

Luke's mind raced in a million directions. There had to be a way to find her. But Seattle? Finding her up near the orchards had been hard enough. How would he ever be able to find her in the largest city of the state?

"I'll go to that hospital. The one Maria is in. I'll wait there until she shows up."

"I'd advise against it. It might make her run again, and there's no telling where she'd go next time. We have to honor her wishes in this."

Luke clenched his fists. *Lord haven't I been patient long enough? Did you send her to me so I would learn the meaning of defeat?*

134

'But why would she run from me? Besides, didn't you tell me she was planning on surgery to remove her scars? Shouldn't that take care of the issue with her face?"

"She gave her savings to Maria's family with instructions they would use it to help her."

Luke would never understand Aimee's rationale. Sure, she demonstrated love and unselfishness in regards to Maria. But what about him? She'd totally ignored his feelings. She'd merely assumed he'd dismiss her for such a vain reason.

Jim interrupted his thoughts. "I'll try to get up there to meet your folks."

"Thanks."

"I can tell you need some time on your knees, so I'll let you go."

The men said goodbye, and Luke wandered into his kitchen to fix himself another lonely meal. He knew he should be on his knees, but what did he have to say to God now? Everything he'd thought God had been telling him blew away in the wind. His dreams ended in the fact that he'd only been indulging in wishful thinking. He'd elevated Aimee to a status she would never live up to. She was no different than the women he knew who spent half their paychecks on clothes, jewelry and makeup. She hadn't really cared for, or trusted him at all.

***

Luke's parents sat on either side of him during the Sunday Christmas service. He'd booked them a room at an exclusive bed and breakfast place a few miles from Wenatchee and they were planning to celebrate Christmas and his birthday together. He glanced at his mother. *They deserve a second honeymoon after all they've been through during Dad's heart attacks.*

Luke had an additional surprise in store for them. He'd given up the lease on his apartment and would be moving back to his hometown to be near them. With no job, no wife on the horizon, and no ministry, there was no reason to stay on in Wenatchee. Luke would be thirty years old the next day. His prayer for a life partner had gone unanswered.

"But I gave you Aimee."

Luke looked over his shoulder to see where the voice had come from. He only saw two rows of teenagers behind him. He turned his attention back to the front of the church, where the worship team had assembled and were hooking up their microphones.

Why did Aimee always seem to invade his thoughts at the wrong time? He'd tried hard not to let his hurt show when around other people, but every reminder of her opened his wounds again.

"Be patient, my son."

The voice again. Was he losing his mind? Had his dreaming finally sent him over the edge? There was no use turning around again. He knew nobody was there. The voice was in his head.

Luke's mom whispered, "Is something wrong, Lukie?"

"No."

"You seem upset. And you keep looking behind you. Are you expecting someone?"

"No. I thought somebody called my name, that's all."

The plaintive introduction to Silent Night, strummed on a lone guitar, filled the room. The lights went down as all the people prepared to celebrate the birth of Christ.

Children's voices, lifted in song, reached his ears from the back of the church. As the music came closer, the congregation rose to their feet. Pastor Greg, a huge smile on his face stood on the platform with the senior pastor, ready to receive the children's choir. Usually they only performed for the Sunday school's Christmas program, but evidently they'd made an exception this time.

Luke strained to see over people's heads. Everyone else did the same thing, blocking his view. He shifted his gaze back to the Pastor Greg, who was looking directly at him with the silliest grin on his face. Then someone clapped, and soon the entire building erupted in applause.

Luke and his parents clapped along with everyone else, even though they still couldn't see the procession. The little parade finally reached the front. All the seats were filled, so the woman leading the band of singers seated them on the carpeted floor directly in front of the first row. Luke could only see the tops of their heads, which were adorned with white and silver garlands.

The clapping continued. "Your church is very proud of their youth." The applause and joyful murmurs from the crowd nearly drowned out his mother's statement.

Greg motioned everyone to be seated. Luke finally got a clear view of the children. He knew some of them! They were from the orchards! No wonder Greg smiled at him. How had they gotten there? Luke no longer offered transportation since they'd begged him not to come anymore since the fire.

Off to the side, a woman stood against one of the pillars holding a little girl's hand. Aimee! With Maria! He'd recognize the color of her long hair anywhere. She turned her head and gazed over the audience as if looking for someone. He saw the scars then. But instead of revulsion or pity, he saw them as evidence of her love for Maria.

Would she see him? Would she run? Luke wanted to leave his seat and go to her in the worst way. Instead he stayed glued to his seat, afraid of chasing her away again.

137

CHAPTER FOURTEEN

The last strains of the old hymn ended and Greg opened his Bible. "We're here to celebrate the birth of our Lord Jesus Christ. It was he who said, *"Suffer the little children to come unto me, and forbid them not: for such is the kingdom of God."*

These children seated on the floor in front of us, are a prime example of who Jesus was talking about. He *wanted* them to come."

Luke vaguely heard what Greg said. He couldn't take his gaze off Aimee. He couldn't get enough of seeing the woman he'd dreamed of, even before he met her.

The pastor looked around the packed sanctuary. "Didn't it do your heart good to see and hear these little ones this morning?"

A chorus of "amen's" answered him.

"I'd especially like to thank Aimee McPherson and her father, Jim, for making this possible." He stopped and waited for the applause to end. "And the parents of these beautiful children, who are standing in the back. Could you all move a little closer together and make room for them to be seated?"

Rustling and whispering came from every corner of the room while people shuffled around to accommodate the guests. Luke kept his eyes on Aimee, who by then had seated herself and Maria on the floor with the other children.

"Now that everyone is settled, I'd like to acknowledge one of our own members, without whom, this special gift to us never would have happened. Luke Forsythe. Would you please stand?"

Luke's dad gave him a little shove. "Go on, son."

He hesitated, fearing Aimee's reaction. But she had to know he was there, right? He stood, carefully avoiding looking directly at her.

Again, the assembly applauded. Luke sat down immediately, still not looking in Aimee's direction.

"Luke came to me some time back, to tell me he had a heart for the farm workers who labor and live in the orchards. He's toiled tirelessly on their behalf, even with some risk to himself. Others of you joined him in this effort. I'm not saying this to embarrass him, but to show you the influence of one man's dream. Don't ever ignore the Lord's prompting. He can use any of us to do great things for His kingdom."

"If any of you would like to join Luke in this endeavor, I'm sure he'll gladly tell you how your can help. Now, let's turn the service back over to our worship team and stand, joining them in praising God for the gift of His Son."

Greg knew about Aimee coming this morning? Luke stole a glance at her. *She's gone!* He stiffened. He should have known she'd run off.

Have faith, my son. I've answered your prayers haven't I?

There it was again--that voice! This time he *knew* it hadn't come from anyone seated nearby. Everyone was busy singing along with the worship team. It had to be . . . the still small voice of God. Shame filled him. He swallowed hard. He hadn't even recognized his Master speaking to him.

The people in his row, to his left, scuffled their feet and moved around, letting more newcomers in. As the disturbance moved closer to where he stood, his heart skipped a beat. Then another.

Aimee moved into the space between him and his dad, and stopped, tucking her hand into his arm. If he'd been a girl, he would have swooned.

The rest of the service passed in a blur. His only recollection was Aimee's hand in his. He could hardly wait for the last song to be over so he could introduce her to his parents. Then he'd get her off somewhere for a long talk. There was so much to say. God had truly answered his

139

prayers. Leaving Wenatchee with his parents was now out of the question. His life stood right next to him.

***

Aimee knew she was taking a chance her heart would be broken if Luke rebuffed her. And why wouldn't he? He'd given her chance after chance to take their relationship to the next level. She wasn't proud of all her past decisions. But hopefully, with God's help, she could start anew.

Only a few weeks ago, hiding out would have been preferable to showing her face in public . . . especially to Luke. Now she saw she'd been guilty of pride. She'd put her needs above Luke's. She'd even jeopardized the arson investigation by not making herself available. Because of her, her father and Luke could have gotten hurt, or worse, when they tried to apprehend that deputy by themselves.

She'd also learned the meaning of forgiveness. Her father had forgiven her. She'd forgiven him and herself, and God's forgiveness through his Son, covered them all.

As she stood next to Luke, her heart overflowed with love for him. Love because of the kind of man he was, and also because he didn't hesitate to pull her close to him when she came and stood by him. The weeks she'd been away seemed to disappear in that moment.

Luke squeezed her hand and when she turned and her gaze met his, his eyes told her everything she needed to know. She saw a thin veil of tears, but also saw something else. Everything was going to be OK.

The music stopped and the congregation sat down. Luke kept hold of her hand, his fingers laced through hers. His touch made it difficult to concentrate on what the pastor was saying, but the love of God for His people came through loud and clear.

When the sermon was over, everyone stood and sang "Oh Holy Night." Luke never let go of her hand once. As they launched into the second verse, everyone reached out to

140

their neighbor until everyone's hands were clasped like a long, unending chain. A lump rose in Aimee's throat as the enormity of the moment took over.

PROLOGUE

Aimee stood in the anteroom at the back of the church, waiting for the first strains of "The Bridal March" Maria stood next to her, dressed in a deep red velvet dress and holding a basket of rose petals. A bandage covered one side of the little girl's face, but at least the burns no longer caused her pain.

Carmelita, Aimee's only attendant, was dressed in a grownup version of the same dress as Maria's.

Her father had paid for everything. Her parents had set aside money for Aimee's college education. When Aimee ran off and began her career without it, Her father had let it sit in the bank drawing interest. The fund had grown enough to pay for the wedding, and Aimee's surgery if she still wanted to have it.

Luke and Aimee had discussed her wish for surgery, but had decided to hold off on that decision. There were many other worthy causes and Aimee wanted the option to help others as the need arose.

Her father moved up beside her. Tears welled in her eyes when she saw how proud he looked to be walking her down the aisle. The music started and she took his arm. Maria and Carmelita entered the sanctuary first. Then it was Aimee's turn.

Her father leaned toward her and spoke into her ear. "You're every bit as beautiful as your mother. She'd be proud of you today."

"Stop it, Daddy. You'll make me cry on my wedding day."

"Tears of joy, Dear."

"You're right. Joy to find the gift of love and to discover the power and depth of it was way more than I'd ever imagined."

Aimee stopped whispering when they rounded the corner and stood poised on the edge of the carpet. The gift she spoke of stood at the very end of the walk she and her father would soon take. Luke's face broke into a smile when he saw her. Her heart jumped at the sight, and as the congregation rose to their feet, she took the first step into their future.

###